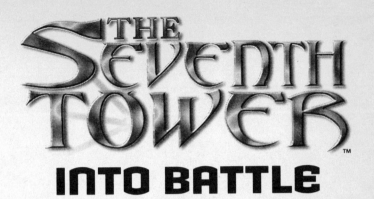

THE SEVENTH TOWER™
INTO BATTLE

by
Garth Nix

www.theseventhtower.com

LUCAS BOOKS

SCHOLASTIC INC.

New York Toronto London Auckland Sydney
Mexico City New Delhi Hong Kong Buenos Aires

ISBN 0-439-17686-7

Copyright © 2001 Lucasfilm Ltd. & TM. All rights reserved. Used Under Authorization.

Cover designed by Joan Moloney. Cover art by Steve Rawlings.

SCHOLASTIC and associated logos are trademarks and/or registered trademarks of Scholastic Inc.

12 11 10 9 8 7 6 5 4 3 2   2 3 4 5 6/0

Printed in the U.S.A.

First Scholastic printing, August 2001

To all the readers who have travelled
with Tal and Milla through four books.
I hope you stay for the complete journey!

·CHAPTER·
⊙ΟΠΕ

High on the road up the Mountain of Light, in a tent made from tightly sewn Wreska hides, Milla sat in a chair carved from the single lower jawbone of an infant Selski. Outside the wind howled, and blown ice and snow struck the tent's walls with a constant rattle.

The bone chair was enormous and made Milla seem smaller than she was, like a child pretending to join her elders. The chair had been carried up the mountain path by eight Shield Maidens, with considerable effort and danger. It was ancient, and the arms, seat, and back were engraved with hundreds of small images from Icecarl history and legend. Next to Milla's hand, for example, there was a thumbnail-sized picture of the fabled Ulla Strong-

Arm wrestling a Merwin, its horn about to be snapped off by the ferocious Icecarl.

Milla felt a twinge in her side as she looked at the tiny picture, the scar aching once again where a Merwin's horn had almost fatally injured her. She knew without a doubt that no one could wrestle a Merwin, but at the same time, she didn't doubt that Ulla Strong-Arm had done it.

Milla looked at some of the other pictures and wondered if the heroes of Icecarl history felt like she did — an imposter who wasn't fit to be the stuff of legend.

She was no longer Milla of the Far-Raiders. She was now Milla Talon-Hand, the Living Sword of Asteyr and War-Chief of the Icecarls. The glowing violet fingernail of magical crystal she wore on her right hand was the legendary weapon of her far ancestor Danir. She was sitting on the ancient Thinking Chair of Grettir. She wore the finest silver Ursek furs. A bone circlet, itself carved with tiny pictures of Icecarl triumph, secured her blond hair in place.

A shield of mirror-bright shell leaned against the throne. It was ancient, too, a relic from distant times when the Icecarls had needed to defend themselves from light magic. Next to it was a Merwin-horn sword. It wasn't the one Milla had left stuck in the shoulder of the Dark Vizier Sushin, back in the Castle, but an older weapon. It still had a faint glow, which would make it effective against Spiritshadows.

Milla sat on the Thinking Chair, wondering what she was doing. She might be called War-Chief, but in practice she spent a lot of time waiting for the Crones to tell her what to do. Since they had bound her with the Prayer of Asteyr she had no choice but to obey, as did her Spiritshadow, Odris.

"It's better than being dead," said that Spiritshadow now, rising up from under the chair to hang in the air in front of Milla's gloomy face.

"Stop knowing what I'm thinking!" snapped Milla, even though she knew it was no use. Odris was linked to her too strongly now, both by the original binding that had been made in the Spirit World of Aenir and by the Prayer of Asteyr. They would be together until one of them died.

"Stop thinking about dying!" Odris snapped back. "I don't know why there's such a fog inside you. You're the War-Chief, the leader of the Expedition against the Castle. Probably the most famous Icecarl alive. They're making up songs about you already. I heard one that goes:

Mighty the one-eyed Merwin   Small the slender
*   Shield Maiden*
Bright the Sunstone's brilliance Darting the
*   dagger drives*
Home it sinks in hoary hide   Milla more than
*   Merwin's match . . .*

"That's all wrong!" interrupted Milla, shaking her head. "I'm not a Shield Maiden and I never will be. Plus, Tal was the one who blinded the Merwin with his Sunstone, not me. And even if I did kill the Merwin, what else have I done right? I broke all the laws, I lost my shadow. I should have been left to die on the Ice."

"You're just sulking because we've had to sit here for too long," said Odris. "Don't worry, the Crones will come up with some sort of airweed soon and then we'll conquer the Castle and send all the Spiritshadows back to Aenir. Then we can go back as well and you can . . . I don't know . . . start a small farm, or get a fishing boat or something. . . ."

"Odris, I'm an Icecarl!" Milla protested. "This is my world. I don't want to live in Aenir. And I am not a farmer or a fisher. I am a warrior!"

"So you should be happy," grumbled Odris. "You make me feel ill with your sadness."

Silence returned, save for the howling of the wind outside. Odris slid back to the floor. Milla brooded on her chair, but only for a few more minutes.

"We have sat here too long," Milla announced.

She leaped up, pulled her heavy outer coat from the back of the chair, and put it on, slipping the white bone mask over her face before raising the hood and pulling it tight. Then she buckled on her sword and slung the mirror-shell shield on her back.

"I take it we're going somewhere?" Odris asked with a sigh. "Can I have some more light?"

Milla raised her hand, and the Sunstone ring on her third finger suddenly shone brightly, eclipsing the greenish light from the moth-lanterns that hung from the massive poles in each corner of the tent.

"Where are we going, by the way?" Odris asked as Milla pulled back the heavy furs that closed the doorway. Together they stepped out into the horizontal waves of wind-driven snow.

"The Crones have had long enough to find airweed," Milla shouted. "I left some at the heatway tunnel entrance. Enough for me to go back through and organize the Underfolk to bring out a whole lot more."

Odris shrugged as she slipped into place at Milla's heels, a shrug that suggested that going back into the Castle through the heatways wouldn't be as easy as Milla made it sound.

At least they were heading in the right direction as far as Odris was concerned. Back to plenty of Sunstone light and Adras, her fellow Storm Shepherd — now also a Spiritshadow.

Odris hadn't wanted to leave the Castle in the first place. But Milla had been determined to warn the Icecarls of the danger to the Veil, not to mention wanting to give herself to the Ice. Fortunately it had all turned out better than Odris had feared.

It took Odris a few seconds to coordinate herself to Milla's quick movements once they were outside. Although the Crones had allowed Odris a limited freedom, ordinary Icecarls were much more comfortable when she tried to behave like a normal shadow. In her natural form in Aenir she was a cloud and could easily shift shape. She had retained this ability to a certain extent as a Spiritshadow, but she was never fast enough to match her movements to Milla's. No one who saw her sliding along behind or to the side, copying Milla's actions a few seconds late, would ever doubt that she was actually a Spiritshadow.

Even with the bright light from Milla's Sunstone it was hard to see the full Icecarl host camped along the road, as the snow was still falling heavily and swirling sideways into the mountain. Every few stretches there would be a moth-lantern or two tied to a bone stake driven into the side of the mountain, and the corner of a tent would become visible, or a stack of supplies.

There were also many Shield Maidens and Icecarl hunters who would suddenly appear out of the whirling snow. Whatever they were doing, they would stop and clap their fists together in greeting as Milla approached. She had to pause and clap her fists in turn, so it took a long time just to walk a hundred stretches from Milla's tent down the road. Eventually she arrived at the point where the entry to the heatway tunnels was marked by two huge flaming tubs of Selski oil.

The entrance was guarded by a full Hand of Shield Maidens in shell-mirror armor. They carried shadowsacks, shadow-bottles, and spears with tips that were heavily coated with luminous algae. The equipment and the luminous algae had all come from secret stores in the Ruin Ship. The Crones had thrown open the Icecarls' ancient arsenal, releasing many weapons that were specifically designed to fight Aeniran shadows.

The Chosen of the Castle had forgotten the ancient war between the Dark World and the creatures of Aenir, but the Icecarl Crones had not. Through the centuries they had maintained both weapons and knowledge, ready for the war they knew must one day resume.

The Shield Maidens clapped their fists together as Milla approached, but Milla was not fooled. There was a reluctance in their greeting — they were wary of her and Odris. She couldn't see their eyes through the amber lenses of their face masks, but she could tell from the set of their heads that they were ready to defend themselves if she went mad and attacked them.

Milla might command the Shield Maidens, but that was never what she wanted. She wanted to be one of them, and still did. But she knew it was impossible. She had lost her shadow, brought a Spirit-shadow to the Ice . . . and she had slain the Shield Mother Arla. There was no going back for her. She could only go forward.

"We greet you, War-Chief," said the Shield Mother of this Hand. Milla didn't know her name. So many Shield Maidens and hunters had come, and even three or four Sword-Thanes. Many more were still on the way across the Ice, though there were already almost two thousand Icecarls camped all along the road from the Ruin Ship up the Mountain of Light. Another thousand or more were kept busy hunting the Ice below for food to feed the host, and there was a continuous line of carriers and carters taking food and supplies between the Ruin Ship below and the various encampments on the road.

"I am going in to the heatways," announced Milla, raising her voice so it would carry over the wind. "Please tell the Crone Malen that I will be some time."

"No need," said a voice beyond the Shield Maidens. A moment later a figure materialized out of the whirling snow. A slim young woman — perhaps a circling older than Milla, who wore the light black furs of a Crone. She carried no weapons and did not wear a face mask, despite the wind and stinging snow. Her eyes were bright blue and glowed with an unnatural light, marking her as a Crone, the blue signifying she was of the youngest of the three orders. In time her eyes would turn silver, and then cloudy and white.

"What do you intend?" asked Malen.

She spoke easily enough, but Milla grimaced as she heard it. Because of the Prayer of Asteyr, she had to obey the commands of the Crones, who spoke with one voice. In this case, it meant obeying the commands of Malen.

The young Crone was bound to stop her, Milla thought. She tensed, trying to resist the command before it came.

"We are taking too long to find a substitute for the Underfolk's airweed," Milla said as calmly as she could. "I left some near the heatway entrance. Using it, I will go back through the tunnels and find the Freefolk rebels. I am sure they will help me bring plenty of airweed back, if we agree to free them from the Chosen when we take the Castle."

Malen listened in silence. Her eyes clouded a little, the luminosity dimming. Milla knew this meant she was communicating with other Crones. They were seeing through her eyes, listening through the young Crone's ears. Any decision that came would be from all the Crones, or at least all of those who chose to participate. It wouldn't be just from Malen.

Even so, Milla almost hated the other girl. She had everything Milla had always wanted. Not to be a Crone, but to have a proper place. To have the respect of the Shield Maidens. To be adored by her clan.

"Yes," Malen said finally. "We have taken too

long, and there is no sign we will succeed in our search for airweed under the Ice. It is best that you find the Freefolk and get them to bring airweed. I will come with you."

"There's not . . ."

Milla started to say "not enough airweed" but the words never came out, because she knew that there was enough airweed for two, if they were careful, and Malen's eyes were fixed on her own. Milla knew the Crone would feel the lie.

"Come on, then," Milla said gruffly.

Milla climbed up to the heatway entrance as the Shield Maidens clapped their fists together again. This time it was more for the Crone, Milla knew. She ignored that, and crawled inside.

11
•

· CHAPTER ·
TWO

Tal settled back into the sarcophagus, the stone cold against his back. Waves of shivering rocked his whole body every few seconds. He kept seeing the beam of light from his Sunstone strike the ceiling. He saw the stone lintel above the door crack and come tumbling down. He saw the steam howling out from the cracked wall.

Most of all, Tal remembered Crow's sudden look of terror as the avalanche of stone, steam, and dust came down upon him.

Crow's face haunted him, but he had not been alone. Tal had almost certainly killed Clovil, and maybe others of Crow's Underfolk gang, and most horribly of all, his own great-uncle Ebbitt. They had all been directly in the path of the falling rocks and the scalding jets of steam. There was no way they could have escaped the collapse of the ceiling and the rupturing of one of the Castle's major steam risers.

It had only happened an hour before, but it was one of the longest hours Tal had ever experienced. He'd tried to stop the falling rocks and the steam but had been driven back. He'd called for help, but no one came. All the Chosen were away. Their bodies might be sleeping in their chambers, but their spirits, their essential selves, were in the Spirit World of Aenir. So there was no one powerful enough to do anything. The Underfolk would arrive eventually, but they could do no more than clean up . . . shut off the steam somewhere down below . . . and dig the bodies out of the rubble.

A thin, squeaky voice interrupted Tal's awful memories. He craned his neck forward to look at the Red Keystone he held in his hand, flat on his chest. It glowed in the darkness of the sarcophagus. Tal concentrated on it, and the image of Lokar, the Guardian of the Red Keystone who was trapped inside the Sunstone, slowly came into focus. She was talking to him, he realized. He should concentrate on what she was saying.

"Tal! Listen . . . you must listen! We must get as

close to the Chosen Enclave as we can," repeated Lokar. "Do you know how to focus on your arrival point in Aenir, Tal?"

"No," mumbled Tal. He knew he should be concentrating on what she was saying, but he couldn't. His head was full of the disaster he had caused. Lokar kept talking at him, telling him how to focus on his Sunstone so that his spirit would cross to the right place in Aenir.

Aenir was the source of Sunstones and Spirit-shadows. It was also, Tal thought bitterly, the source of all his troubles. He had unwittingly gotten caught up in an age-old struggle between the people of the Dark World — the Chosen and the Icecarls — and the strange creatures of the Spirit World of Aenir. His enemy Sushin was undeniably an agent of the shadows of Aenir, and had trapped Tal's father inside the Orange Keystone, poisoned his mother into a coma, imprisoned his younger brother, Gref, and put his very small sister, Kusi, into the "care" of his awful cousins Lallek and Korrek.

"So close, so close, yet far, very far," muttered Lokar, her voice so strange Tal wasn't sure who she was talking to. Then her voice snapped back to its normal, strident tone. Tal!" Lokar ordered. "There's no time to waste! We must get to the Empress and report on the unlocked Keystones!"

Tal nodded weakly, but he didn't do anything. Something squirmed at the edge of his vision and he flinched, until he realized it was his Spiritshadow, Adras. Adras had been a Storm Shepherd in Aenir, a mighty creature of cloud and air. Normally he would be a very strong Spiritshadow in the Dark World. But he had been starved of light and almost destroyed when Tal had incorrectly created a miniature veil to hide them from hostile Spiritshadows. It had worked, but Tal had never cast one before and had accidentally worked Adras into the Veil. Without any light at all, Adras had shrunk and withered away to almost nothing. Even now, he was very weak.

"Odris!" whispered Adras, close to Tal's ear. Odris was his fellow Storm Shepherd, a companion to the Icecarl Milla, who had left the Castle and gone out onto the Ice. "We should go to Odris. She will help us."

"The Empress," repeated Lokar. "The Empress! The Empress! We must cross to Aenir and inform the Empress! We must! We must —"

"Shut up!" Tal burst out. Why couldn't they be

15

quiet, just for a minute? He needed to lie there in silence, with just the comforting orange glow of his Sunstone ring mixed with the steady crimson pulse of light from the Red Keystone.

Surprisingly, Adras and Lokar both shut up. Tal lay there, breathing quietly, every now and then pressing his hands against the stone lid of the sarcophagus above his head. Pressing hard against the lid released some of the tension inside him.

He still couldn't get that awful frozen second of Crow's face and the falling rock out of his mind. But he finally felt strong enough to make a firm decision. They would cross to Aenir, find the Empress, and tell her everything. He would make sure that she used the Violet Keystone, the strongest and most important stone, to release his father from the Orange Keystone. Then Tal could tell him everything and he would take over and sort everything out.

Tal felt a little better as he made the decision, until a small voice inside his head reminded him that no one could make Ebbitt and Crow and the others alive again.

"It was Crow's own fault!" Tal said suddenly. Somehow getting angry made him feel better. His head still hurt where Crow had hit him. The Underfolk boy had stolen the Red Keystone, too. If Crow hadn't hit him and taken the Keystone, nothing would have happened. He would still be alive, and so would Ebbitt, Clovil, Ferenc, and Inkie.

"It was his fault," Tal repeated. Crow had started it. The rock fall was an accident that never would have happened otherwise.

·CHAPTER· THREE

"I will go to the Empress," Tal declared as he stared into the Red Keystone. He could see Lokar in the center of the jewel, the small woman looked like she was treading water, her hands and feet in constant movement. Her Spiritshadow, a hopping Leaper-beast, circled her, never stopping. They were both prisoners in the Keystone, trapped there when the stone was unlocked. They could not be released except with Lokar's own Sunstone or the Violet Keystone of the Seventh Tower.

"Good! Oh, good! Excellent!" babbled Lokar. "To make sure we come out close to the Chosen Enclave, you must first fix an image of the place in your head. Then you need to hold that picture there as you recite the Way to Aenir and concentrate on the correct colors. You do . . . you do know the Way to Aenir? Please, you must . . ."

"Of course I know," said Tal, though he didn't know how to transfer to a particular spot. He thought about it for a second. Of course he could do it. He was better at Light Magic now than most adult Chosen. If he hadn't been he would be dead by now.

He had to pick the right part of the Enclave for his arrival. They would have to be careful to avoid being seen. Since the Day of Ascension had just happened, all the Chosen would be in Aenir. Presumably that would include Sushin. As the Dark Vizier, he was able to command any other Chosen in the name of the Empress. There were also a lot of Chosen who willingly followed Sushin, or were duped into obeying him. Probably none of them knew that Sushin was secretly a servant of the free shadows of Aenir, and that his real aim was to destroy the Veil that protected the Dark World from the Sun and from the shadows of Aenir.

Milla thought Sushin *was* some sort of shadow, one who had taken on flesh, but Tal wasn't sure about that.

"Where do you think we should arrive?" Tal asked.

"Soon!" snapped Lokar. "Oh, where? Where? The rim. The rim of the crater, at night."

"At night?" asked Tal. "You mean I can visualize a time as well?"

"Yes," replied Lokar. "Yes. Two deep breaths. One. Two. Where was I? Besides *here*. Yes. Within a day or so. I do not know what would happen if you tried to cross too far into Aenir's future."

"Where do we go if it is not yet night in Aenir?"

"Who knows? Our bodies sleep here, and our spirits arrive there. We will not notice if our spirits spend time somewhere in between. It doesn't matter!"

Tal didn't like the thought of that. But he had decided.

"Visualize," said Lokar. "Hurry. Oh, darkness take you! Think! Think of the Enclave. Pick a spot where you have spent time, that you know well. Remember it in detail. Paint a picture in your head. . . ."

Tal let his head fall back. Lokar's increasingly shrill voice dropped away to the distant buzz of a tunnel-gnat.

He thought of the Chosen Enclave. He saw it in his mind, imagined it as a Storm Shepherd might see it from high overhead. The vast volcanic crater, the rim rising up a thousand stretches above the Plain of Thorns. On the inside of the rim, a lesser fall, only five or six hundred stretches down to the lake that filled the crater. But this was no ordinary lake. It was not water but a mixture of fine gray ash and millions upon millions of tiny clear crystals.

Strange creatures lived in the ash lake. Most were unknown, though some of the shallower regions had been netted over the years, with the catch made to serve as Spiritshadows back in the Castle.

Sushin had originally had a lake-dweller Spiritshadow, a tall, thin creature with an armored shell and a snapping beak. But Sushin had a different Spiritshadow now, another sign of his treachery and alliance with the creatures of Aenir. Chosen did not change their Spiritshadows.

Tal quickly concentrated, remembering details of the Enclave. The Chosen in Aenir stayed in houses built on stilts across the Lake of Ash, houses joined by raised walkways that kept them safely out of reach of the lake-dwellers.

In the very center of the lake there was a real island, rather than a platform made by the Chosen. Protected by stone walls and Sunstone wards, the island was the Empress's Aeniran residence. It had gardens and a palace. It was not open to other Chosen and was not joined to the network of raised pathways and bridges.

Tal thought about arriving on the Empress's island. But he had only seen it from a distance, from high on the crater wall. He couldn't visualize any details because he didn't know any.

He also had better not arrive on a walkway or house. It would be too easy to be seen. Lokar was right, the crater rim would be the best. But where on the crater rim?

Tal remembered climbing up with his parents as a very young boy, before Gref was born. He remembered grizzling and complaining at the steepness of the path, until his father picked him up and piggybacked him most of the way.

But his clearest memory was from the year before. With a bunch of other boys he had climbed to the Hanging Rock to watch some older Chosen light-diving.

The Hanging Rock was a tongue of stone that projected from the crater rim, in toward the lake. It was at least fifty stretches long, a strange, seemingly unsupported platform that was perfect for light-diving. If anywhere could be considered perfect for light-diving, that is. It was a dangerous sport, frowned upon by senior Chosen. Any child who attempted it, rather than a Full Chosen, would automatically gain four Deluminents . . . if they survived. Four Deluminents was more than halfway to the disgrace of demotion, the beginning of a slide that might end in Red or even the white robes of Underfolk.

Light-diving was simple enough. The Chosen divers would weave themselves a rope of light, tie one end around their ankles and the other end to the "anchor hole" in the Hanging Rock. Then they would simply dive off, down toward the lake. If the lightrope was made properly, they would plummet down about two-thirds of the way, then suddenly rebound and bounce up and down for a while. Once they'd come to a stop, it was usually a simple matter to shrink the rope and be drawn back up.

If the rope wasn't properly made, the Chosen diver might fall into the ash, and drown or get eaten by something. Sometimes, less fatally but more embarrassingly, the lightrope wouldn't shrink, and the diver would be left dangling upside down below the Hanging Rock until friends came to the rescue.

The Hanging Rock would be ideal, Tal thought. He would time it so he arrived at dusk. Then he could sneak down the path at night, and onto the network of bridges and walkways. There were some boats on the lake, and he would steal one of those to get to the Empress's island.

Tal fixed the image of the Hanging Rock in his mind, with the red light of the setting sun just upon it. He could see the Rock and the lake below, the crater wall stretching away to either side to circle around in the distance. It was all very clear in his head.

Tal raised his Sunstone and called forth the first of the colors that would begin his transfer. At the same time, he began to recite the Way to Aenir, his words and the colors from the stone mixing together. He felt the color spread across his skin, felt the difference as Red gave way to Orange and then Yellow.

The inside of the stone sarcophagus faded away, to be replaced by swirling colors. Bright rainbows washed across Tal, blurring into each other as each new one passed.

All the way through, he kept the image of the Hanging Rock in his head, with the sunlight just beginning to fall upon it.

Tal was on his way to Aenir. Whether he'd made a good decision or not, he had chosen his cards. Now he would have to play the beast he had created.

·CHAPTER·
FOUR

A heavy outer coat lay a few paces inside the heatway. It was Tal's coat, where they had left it the first time Milla had entered the Castle. That felt like a lifetime ago, or a dream. Milla had been a different person, honored to be going on an adventure, to get a new Sunstone for her clan. Now she no longer belonged to the clan of the Far-Raiders and everything had changed.

"Hurry up!" whispered Odris. "The Crone is stuck outside."

Milla jumped forward and hurried along the heatway. She hadn't realized she'd actually stopped and was touching Tal's coat. This wasn't how a Shield Maiden behaved. She might have been surprised by an enemy! Even though she wasn't a Shield Maiden she should still try to behave like one.

The airweed was farther along the passage. A long stalk of it lay on the floor. Milla picked it up and examined the four bulbous nodules of air that were left. She had used only one nodule on the way out. Even though it had been the biggest, there should still be plenty left for the two of them to make it through.

Taking out her new knife of golden metal — yet another treasure from the Ruin Ship — Milla carefully cut the strand of airweed in half. Handing two of the four nodules to Malen, she explained how to use them.

"When the time comes, Odris will warn us to use the airweed. You must make a tiny hole at the end, where it is softest, and then press your finger on it. Keeping your finger over the hole, put your mouth onto the airweed as if you were a baby suckling milk, and breathe in. Breathe out through your nose. Keep your finger pressed tight over the hole whenever you are not taking a breath."

Milla demonstrated, without actually cutting the nodule. Malen copied her.

"You do have a knife, don't you?" asked Milla. She couldn't see one, nor see the telltale signs of one hidden in a sleeve or boot.

"Yes," said Malen. She looked at Tal's coat. "Do we leave our outer coats here?"

Milla nodded and started to shrug her coat off. The heatways were aptly named. This tunnel and the network of others like it were actually inspection tunnels for the Castle's heating system. It used lava to heat great lakes of water, and the steam was piped throughout the more than a hundred levels and seven towers of the vast building. Unfortunately, over the centuries the lava had broken out of its assigned channels and had invaded some of the inspection tunnels. That was where the bad air came from.

"Odris, go first," Milla ordered.

"Do this, do that," grumbled Odris. "You might be War-Chief of the Icecarls but you're not War-Chief of the Storm Shepherds."

"You need to go first so you can warn me about the bad air," said Milla patiently.

"How can it tell?" asked Malen.

"It!" exclaimed Odris. "How would you like to be called 'it'?"

"She can taste it," Milla answered. "Odris was a Storm Shepherd in Aenir. They have a particular affinity for air, even as Spiritshadows."

Malen nodded, but she didn't answer Odris, or otherwise acknowledge her. Odris stood waiting, puffing herself up to her full size, a huge shadow that completely filled the tunnel.

"Odris, it would please me if you go ahead," said Milla wearily. It was clear that Malen was not going to lower herself to talk to a free shadow.

"Tell *it* to keep *its* distance," hissed Odris, pointing a puffy finger at Malen. Then she turned and started off down the heatway. She shrunk herself at the same time, her shadowflesh becoming darker and denser.

Milla followed her, ignoring the Crone. She would follow or not. Milla was already remembering all the twists and turns of the heatway passages. Tal had found a map the first time through, and she had committed every turn to memory. Coming out she had reversed it and now must reverse it again. There were more than a hundred turns and several climbs to recall, and she had to get it right. A wrong turning or other mistake could plunge them down into the lava flows or the boiling reservoirs.

Despite the increasing heat, Milla kept up a punishing pace, first in a hunched-over walk and then at a crawl as the ceiling lowered. Odris was often only a few steps ahead of her, and Malen was often ten or even twenty stretches behind. Milla knew the Crone would have had no experience of such heat, and was obviously finding it a struggle. But Malen did not complain. All she did was undo the lacings at her throat and sleeves.

Soon they had to resort to breathing through dampened rags, as the heat continued to build. Still Milla kept on, occasionally pausing to think about the next turning before continuing forward. Her Sunstone lit up the tunnel ahead and also provided Odris with a source of strength.

After a few hours they came to the broken skeleton where Milla and Tal had found a Sunstone that Tal's great-uncle Ebbitt had later split in two. Later, on the way back, Milla had found the strange fingernail that she now knew as the Talon of Danir among the bones.

Milla paused before the skeleton and held her Sunstone high. Malen came up close, and they both gazed down upon the bones.

"This is where you found the Sunstone and the Talon," said Malen. "I wonder who bore them? I do not think the bones are particularly old."

Milla scowled. She hadn't noticed before, but the bones were not as ancient as she had always thought. Trust a Crone — this Crone — to instantly recognize something that might be important.

"Tal said he must have been a Chosen," Milla said. "He wore the Sunstone on a ring."

There was no room for Malen to get past Milla to the main skeleton, but the Crone reached out and picked up a bone that had been scattered farther along. She tapped it against the wall, then pulled out a small sharp stone from her sleeve and pared off a sliver.

"Not more than a hundred circlings," Malen pronounced after examining the sliver. "And not less than fifty. I wonder who could have been wearing the Talon of Danir as recently as that?"

Milla shrugged. The question was of no importance to the immediate task. The skeleton was a pile of bones, and bones could not speak.

"The bad air will probably begin soon," Milla said. "Be ready with your airweed."

Malen nodded. Milla gestured Odris to go on. But the Spiritshadow did not move. Instead she held up one puffy hand and cocked her head to one side.

"Wait," she whispered. "Someone comes. There is movement in the air."

Milla reacted instantly, focusing on her Sunstone to dim it to a weak glow. Then she eased her sword in its scabbard, for a quick draw. Behind her, she heard Malen draw in a nervous breath.

They waited in the near darkness for what felt like a long time but wasn't, before a faint light appeared in the distance. It was not even and bright like a Sunstone, or the red glow of the lava, but a flickering yellow.

Milla and Malen lay completely still, close to the floor. Odris slid up against the ceiling and pressed herself there. All of them looked forward.

The yellow light grew brighter. Milla saw two men in white Underfolk robes crawling down the tunnel. They each carried an Underfolk lamp of the type Milla had seen before, simple globes of unbreakable crystal filled with mineral fuel and topped with a wick.

The lamps shed only a narrow circle of light around the men. It also blinded them to what lay ahead.

The yellow light flickered as the Underfolk crawled, but there were more shadows around the men than could be explained by that. Milla tensed as she realized that the men were being followed by two . . . no, three . . . Spiritshadows. Thin, thorny Spiritshadows, not of any kind Milla had ever seen. They were about the same size as the Underfolk, but had six legs, razored and bulbous bodies, and long thin heads that ended in what would probably be a sharp spike or bloodsucking proboscis in their native Aeniran form.

The Underfolk paused to take breaths from air-weed nodules they had slung around their necks. But the Spiritshadows didn't let them take more than one. Their forelegs whipped the men about the shoulders. Milla saw their shadowflesh get darker and denser and the Underfolk flinch under the blows.

These were free shadows, Milla realized. They were using the Underfolk to provide the light they needed. If only the men realized, they could blow out their lanterns and the Spiritshadows would be helpless. But then, down here, so would the Under-folk. And the Spiritshadows might not fade fast enough. . . .

The Underfolk started crawling again. Thoughts flashed through Milla's mind. She had her Sunstone, but didn't really know how to use it properly against Spiritshadows. Her Merwin-horn sword would cut them. Odris could probably outfight one or two of them. The Crone might also be of some use. The Crones did seem to have some tricks they could use against shadows.

The Underfolk kept crawling on. The Spirit-shadows followed them, but not closely. They kept flitting from side to side, thrusting their shadow proboscises into cracks in the walls and ceiling, reaching out with their forelegs.

"They are looking for something," whispered Malen, just as Milla had the same thought.

Milla looked down at the Talon of Danir on her finger. It was glowing violet and gold. When she had fought the Shield Mother Arla, it had suddenly extended and mortally wounded Milla's opponent.

Milla closed her fist to hide the glow of the Talon.

"When they get close, we will attack," she whispered. "The shadows, not the Underfolk."

·CHAPTER·
FIVE

Tal blinked and opened his eyes. As he always did when he arrived in Aenir he felt lighter, less substantial. The first thing he did was look down at himself. Sure enough, his skin had gained the peculiar glow that all Dark Worlders had on Aenir. He knew that he was also shorter and slighter, another effect of the transfer.

Tal looked around, his eyes adjusting to the twilight. It was exactly as he'd pictured it. He stood on the end of the Hanging Rock, high above the Lake of Ash. Out on the lake there was the Empress's island and then, in a semicircle around it, hundreds of Chosen houses, all built high on stilts and joined by narrow bridges and raised walkways.

The anchor hole was near his feet. He could see through it, see the lake far below.

"I've done it!" he exclaimed. There was a red glow in the distance, behind the far crater wall, the sun setting. He had timed it exactly. Soon the last light would fade and he could sneak down the path behind him.

"Adras, I've done it!" he said again.

There was no reply. Puzzled, Tal looked around. There was no sign of the Storm Shepherd. But Tal knew he had to be there. They were inextricably bound together. Adras *couldn't* have been left behind. He'd die in the dark sarcophagus without Tal's Sunstone light!

A faint cry sounded above him. Tal looked up and sighed in relief. Adras was high above him, a faint white speck in the darkening sky. He was still only a third his normal size, but he was no longer a shadow. Like Tal, he had been transformed, in this case back to his natural form, the puffy cloud-flesh of a Storm Shepherd.

"Water," called Adras, his voice thin and high, like the wind blowing between the cracks of a house. "I must find water. I will return!"

He rose up higher then, and Tal felt a pang in his stomach. It wasn't exactly painful, but it wasn't pleasant, either. He knew it would last until Adras came back, and that the Storm Shepherd would also feel it. They could not stay very far apart for too long.

He looked down again, and realized he was still clenching his fist. He opened it and looked at the Red Keystone. As before, Lokar swam into view as he concentrated upon the stone's sparkling depths.

"We're here," announced Tal. "On the Hanging Rock, at dusk."

"Good," replied Lokar. Her voice was almost a sob. "Oh, I will soon be free of this accursed prison! The Empress will use the Violet Keystone to release me!"

"Is it . . . is it that bad in there? Does it hurt?" asked Tal. He wasn't really thinking of Lokar. His thoughts were with his father, Rerem, trapped inside the Orange Keystone.

Lokar laughed, a laugh tinged with hysteria.

"Hurt? It doesn't hurt. Yet I cannot rest, I cannot sleep, I cannot stop this endless circling inside the stone. Unless someone speaks from outside, there is only my Spiritshadow and me, surrounded by silence. Years and years and years of silence. Is it any surprise that I have been mad?"

Tal stared down at her. Suddenly taking her advice didn't seem so sensible. Lokar said she had been mad. What if she still was?

"Speak!" ordered Lokar. "Speak! Tell me what is happening outside!"

"Uh, nothing really."

Tal stumbled over the words. He didn't know what to say. "Um, Adras has flown off to find some water. I'm going to wait until it's a bit darker and start down the path."

He looked up as he spoke, to see how much light was left. To his surprise, the light on the horizon was brighter than before. It was also less red. Tal stared at it, not listening to the buzzing voice of Lokar.

It took him a full two seconds to realize he'd made a dreadful mistake.

It wasn't dusk.

It was dawn.

In a few minutes, the sun would rise above the crater wall. He would be easily seen on the Hanging Rock, or heading down the path. Sushin's followers, or even just some concerned Chosen, would spot him for sure.

"I made a mistake! It's dawn!" he gabbled to the Keystone. Without waiting for an answer, he tied the stone into the corner of his sleeve and pulled it tight, so there was no chance it could be lost. He already had his two vials of water-spider antidote tied in the other sleeve.

There was only one thing Tal could do to avoid detection and capture. He must weave a lightrope within the next few minutes and dive down to the Lake of Ash. But unlike the regular light-divers who returned to the Hanging Rock by shrinking their ropes, he would have to try and get as close to the ash as possible, cut himself free, and swim ashore.

Tal knew the principles of lightropes. A red strand for strength, a yellow strand for flexibility, and an indigo strand to keep it all together. A few months ago he had never even handled light above the yellow spectrum, but now he didn't hesitate. He would even use violet if he had to.

Tal lifted his Sunstone ring and concentrated on it. A thick line of red light spilled out of the Stone and fell down, coiling as it fell. Tal kept it going and added a yellow strand, thicker than the red. Then came the indigo, winding about the two other strands. The complete rope kept falling and coiling, and Tal realized he had another problem.

He didn't know how long to make the lightrope. If it was too short he'd just bounce up and down and end up hanging too far above the ash to safely drop. If it was too long he'd dive deep into the ash and even though he'd probably bounce out several times, the initial impact would probably kill him.

Desperately he tried to remember watching other light-divers. He tried to recall conversations he'd overheard. Was it three hundred and fifty stretches? It was three hundred and something . . . three hundred and sixty?

Tal decided shorter was safer than longer. Better to be captured alive dangling above the Lake of Ash than killed. He decided on three hundred and fifty. Allowing five stretches for the loose ends before the lightrope wove together, he was almost there.

A thin sliver of sun was already poking over the far crater wall. Behind him, there was sunlight on the closer wall, about fifty stretches above him. He could see the line of sunlight falling every minute, creeping closer down to him.

Tal twisted his hand and directed the end of the rope through the anchor hole, directing the light so it shot under the Hanging Rock and back over to re-join itself below his hand. Tal pulled back as if he were lifting a weight, tightening the loop until the rope was fast against the rock. Then he cut it off with a thought and went forward to pick up the other end. After cutting off the loose strands with a fine ray of Red light, he used two fingers of Indigo light to tie the lightrope securely around his ankles.

The sunlight hit the top of his head. Tal took a deep breath and shuffled to the very edge of the Hanging Rock.

He looked down. The lake was a long, long way down. The Chosen houses and the walkways between them were tiny.

Sunlight touched his eyes.

Tal shut them firmly and leaned forward. For a moment he hung on the very edge of the Hanging Rock.

Then he toppled forward and fell straight down, the lightrope rippling out behind him.

·CHAPTER·
SIX

The Underfolk crawled closer. The free Spirit-shadows followed right behind them. As the light from the lanterns illuminated a stray bone from the skeleton, the Underfolk stopped and pointed. Instantly, the three Spiritshadows swarmed forward, obviously excited. The Underfolk shuddered as the Spiritshadows slid over and past them, cold shadowflesh chilling them through their robes.

The lead Spiritshadow touched the bone with its proboscis, then with its two front claws. Then it looked at the others, and all three briefly touched their forelegs.

At that moment, while they were distracted, Milla attacked.

She lunged forward in a crouch, her hand extended, trusting that the Talon of Danir would do whatever it did automatically.

She intended to use the glowing fingernail to cut the closest Spiritshadow. But as she leaped forward, the Talon extended itself, until it was as long as her forearm. Bright violet sparks showered from the end, and a long plume of violet light shot out like a whip — a whip of light at least three stretches long.

Milla brought her hand down toward the Spiritshadow, and the whip of light shot around and became a lasso. Without conscious direction from Milla, it settled over the head of the Spiritshadow and pulled tight. It went through the shadowflesh like a wire through cheese, cutting the Spiritshadow's head off in a single sharp action.

Milla flicked the lasso at the next one, and the same thing happened. As she flicked it at the third and last Spiritshadow, the other two were picking up their separated heads and then trying to reconnect them, as they scuttled as fast as they could back down the tunnel.

The third Spiritshadow was quicker and the lasso missed. But before it could attack Milla, the violet streamer undid itself and the free end whipped out to slice through the Spiritshadow's forelegs. The creature crashed to the floor, and wriggled backward, sliding over the Underfolk, who had pressed themselves facedown on the floor. It halted for a moment, then scuttled away.

Odris had rushed forward to grab the shadow, but as she reached out, the light from the Talon whipped back toward her. Instantly, Milla threw her hand the other way, slapping her palm against the wall.

The whip missed Odris by a finger-width.

"Careful!" boomed Odris. She sounded scared.

Milla was shaken, too. She held her hand against the wall, until the violet stream of light slowly ebbed back into the Talon, and it shrank back to its regular size.

43

"I didn't know it did that," said Milla. No wonder Danir had been such a fearsome warrior, her legend lasting thousands of years. She had worn one of these magical fingernails on each hand.

"Interesting," said Malen. "The Talon seems to act of its own accord against shadows."

"I'm staying back here, then," said Odris, "until you learn to control it."

Milla nodded and cautiously drew her hand back from the wall. The Talon didn't do anything. Perhaps it only worked when she wanted to fight. She would have to be careful to make sure Odris wasn't nearby when she did. In a way it was like being a Wilder, one of the berserk warriors that occasionally emerged in the clans. You had to stay clear of them when they fought, until the blood-craze left them and they knew friend from foe.

"You can get up now," said Milla to the two Underfolk. "Well, you can crouch, anyway."

She crawled up to them, but they didn't move. Milla raised her Sunstone and light flared, the brightness washing out the yellow glow of the lanterns.

"You can . . ." Milla started to say again. Then she scowled and reached forward to touch the closest man. He didn't move.

Milla felt for a pulse in his neck and then repeated the action with the other one.

Neither one had a pulse.

"They're dead," she said slowly. "But I don't see how."

She shuffled up between the two bodies. Only then did she see that they each had a tiny wound in their back of the head. A wound about the same size as one of the Spiritshadow's proboscis.

"The last one must have stabbed them as it passed," Milla said.

She felt strangely affected by their deaths. Death was no stranger to her, even sudden, unexpected, and violent death. But somehow this felt worse than the accidents she had seen, or the fatal encounters with the wild beasts of the Ice.

It took her a moment to realize what it was.

"Shadows have killed," she said slowly. "I do not think I believed it was possible before."

"It is not only possible, it has happened many times before, long ago," said Malen. "The ancient war has begun again. We know it, as do the shadows of Aenir, even if the Chosen do not. You realize what those shadows were looking for?"

Milla nodded.

"The Talon," she said, looking back at the skeleton. "And perhaps the Sunstone. The Spiritshadows expected to find the man's remains — or what he carried — to be here somewhere. That is why they were searching so carefully."

"They have reason to be afraid of the Talon," said Malen. "I wonder how much a shadow can be cut before it cannot repair itself?"

"This is a very morbid conversation," said Odris. "Personally, I don't want to find out."

No one spoke for a moment. Milla carefully rolled the two Underfolk over to look at their faces and fix them in her mind, so she could describe them later and find out their names. She wondered if the

Freefolk would know them. Perhaps they were close family. Certainly they would be someone's brothers, or uncles, or fathers.

"I do not know what the Underfolk do with their dead," Milla said finally, as she folded their arms across their chests and carefully opened their eyes wide so they might see their way ahead. "The Chosen trap them in stone boxes."

"I have spoken to Crone Mother Panul," said Malen. "I have told her the turnings. She will send Shield Maidens to take these Underfolk out and give them to the Ice. There is no likelihood of bad air between here and the outside, is there?"

"I don't think so," replied Milla. She gestured down the tunnel. "It lies ahead. Tell Panul they should take the airweed these men carried. Tell her how to use it."

Malen nodded. Her eyes clouded as she joined the mass mind of the Crones.

Milla looked away, at the tunnel stretching out ahead. The Spiritshadows would have spread the alarm. They would not know who they encountered, but they would tell of the deadly whip of violet light.

Many shadows might be gathering now in the lower Underfolk levels, waiting for Milla, Malen, and Odris. The Chosen should all be in Aenir, but even if they weren't, Milla wasn't afraid of them. They had lived too easy lives. They were not warriors.

Free shadows from Aenir were a different matter.

"Come," she said. "We must hurry. The enemy now knows that the evening breeze brings raiders down upon the ship."

"What?" asked Odris. "Which raiders? What ship?"

"It's only a saying," said Milla. "Anyone would think you were Adras."

"Adras is gone," sighed Odris. "Gone to Aenir, back to being a Storm Shepherd."

"Gone?" asked Milla. "But Tal was to get the Red Keystone. He shouldn't be in Aenir."

"Maybe he isn't," said Odris mournfully. "Maybe . . . maybe he's dead, and Adras was released. I don't know."

"When did this happen? Why didn't you tell me?"

Odris shrugged. "Three sleeps ago. I heard his farewell upon the wind. You were sulking on your stupid chair."

"You must tell me matters of importance," Milla said angrily. "I bet he's got himself into trouble again."

"Adras?"

"No, Tal! Come on!"

·CHAPTER·
SEVEN

Tal plummeted down, the lightrope spilling out behind him. Down and down he fell, his arms spread wide, his head back. He saw the Lake of Ash below, coming closer and closer and closer, and still he fell, the lightrope running free.

Any moment, the rope would run out and he would bounce back, but the moment didn't come and the lake was so close, only ten or twenty stretches below — and this time Adras wasn't nearby to catch him!

The rope was too long. He was going to hit the lake!

Tal wrapped his arms around his head and screwed his eyes shut. He felt his stomach stay behind as his fall was suddenly arrested. He opened his eyes and saw the surface of the lake just beyond his reach — and then he was hurtling up again as the rope jerked him back.

His stomach felt like it was determined to stay on the surface of the lake as Tal bounced up and down. When he finally came to rest, he was hanging about four stretches above the surface of the ash and sixty stretches from the shore.

The surface of the lake was quite smooth. Even though it looked completely gray higher up, from this distance all the clear crystals allowed Tal to see a little way under the surface. It was like looking into very cloudy water. Not that there was anything to see, which was a good sign. He didn't want to see anything there.

Flipping himself up, Tal grabbed the rope. He used his Sunstone to unravel the indigo binding thread. He hung from his hands for a moment, then let himself go. Above him, his lightrope dissipated into the air.

Tal fell straight down into the strange fluid of the lake, only remembering to hold his arms out at the last moment, so his head didn't go under.

The mixture of ash and tiny crystals almost felt like water, but it was warm and dry, and it was much harder to move through. Luckily, it was easier to stay afloat.

Tal started swimming to the shore immediately. It would be daylight throughout the crater soon, and he had to find somewhere to hide.

He was halfway to the shore when he noticed that there was another noise beside the curious rustling sound of his own swimming. A sound that he could feel as a vibration through the ash, as well as hear. It was coming from behind him, so he rolled over to look, while continuing with a fairly clumsy back-stroke.

At first he couldn't see anything. Then a large and highly unwelcome shape briefly surfaced about a hundred stretches away, before disappearing again.

Tal saw a great long back of serrated blue and red scales, accompanied by the brief flash of a huge mouth surrounded by four long, questing tendrils.

Suddenly Tal's arms started thrashing through the ash with new strength and speed.

He knew what he'd seen. It was a Kerfer, one of the great carnivores of the lake. A creature played in Beastmaker for Strength or Special. Its Special ability lay in its six feathery tentacles. Four were several times longer than a man and sensed vibration and movement. Two were shorter, but oozed a paralyzing venom.

Tal looked again. The Kerfer briefly broached the surface, tentacles rising into the air before they splashed down ahead of its body. It had closed the distance between them by half in only a few seconds. He had no chance of outswimming it.

The Chosen boy stopped swimming, though his feet trod the ash to keep him afloat. He raised his Sunstone ring and concentrated on it. Red light grew in intensity there, until it was almost blinding.

A tentacle rose up out of the ash just a stretch away. One of the sensing tentacles — but the paralyzing tentacle would not be far behind.

Tal waited. The tentacle quested forward and touched his chest. He flinched, and it recoiled. Then came the target Tal had been waiting for. The Kerfer breached again, and he saw its cavernous mouth, a mouth lined with wriggling cilia instead of teeth.

Tal fired the Red Ray of Destruction at the highest intensity he could summon, straight between the monster's jaws.

Light exploded everywhere, the crystals in the ash picking up and multiplying the red flash. Tal was momentarily blinded. Something hit him, and he screamed, thinking it was the paralyzing tentacle. Ash filled his mouth. The Kerfer had reared up and splashed down, creating a huge wave.

Tal's vision cleared as he spat out ash. For a moment he couldn't orient himself, couldn't see the shore or the monster. Then he saw the Kerfer floating on the surface, its tentacles limp. It was either stunned or dead.

Tal didn't wait around to see which it was. He struck out for the shore as fast as he could.

He climbed up onto a beach of more solid ash. He didn't look behind until he was safely on rock and a good twenty stretches from the lake. Then he turned around, his Sunstone ready, in case the Kerfer was going to drag itself after him.

It wasn't. As Tal watched, the inert creature bobbed under once, then twice, as if something was nibbling on it.

Something was. Tal couldn't help retreating even farther from the lake as the whole Kerfer — a creature that would weigh ten times as much as Tal — disappeared with a sudden *pop*, leaving a deep whirlpool in the lake that was easily fifty stretches in diameter.

Tal shuddered. He was glad he hadn't encountered whatever *that* was instead of the Kerfer.

Now his priority was to find somewhere to hide, so he wasn't exposed out here in the sun. The crater wall had lots of caves. But was there one close by?

He ran toward the wall, jumping from one tumbled rock to another. There were a few promising patches of dark shadow ahead. One of them should be a cavemouth. And apart from the lake, the Chosen made sure that there were no creatures within the crater itself. So there should be no danger from a Cavernmouth, or any other of the horrendous inhabitants of the rest of Aenir.

At least, Tal thought, there shouldn't be any danger. But then he'd never gone into any caves that weren't on the path . . .

·CHAPTER·
EIGHT

No Spiritshadows lay in wait for Milla, Odris, and Malen. As Milla cautiously crept out into the lowest of the Underfolk levels she wondered whether the three spiky-snouted Spiritshadows had perished from their wounds or lack of light. Or perhaps they had gotten lost, or had not reported their find.

Whatever had happened, she was grateful. Not that she was afraid of fighting shadows. She simply preferred the battle to be fought when she had a great host of specially armed and armored Icecarls behind her.

This trip was a raid, and airweed was the prize they sought. In fact, they could not return without it, for their own supply was now exhausted.

It took Milla a moment to reorient herself as

Malen climbed out behind her. She had taken extra care to memorize all the twists and turns of the heatways, but had not paid particular attention to the Underfolk levels. Even so, she had subconsciously mapped it all in her head, as any good Ice-carl would do.

"This way," she said decisively, pointing down the plain, whitewashed corridor. Its ceiling held occasional, weak, undersized Sunstones, and consequently the hallway had many shadows. Natural shadows, Milla was pretty sure, though she was ready to strike with the Talon if necessary.

Odris noticed the tension in Milla's hand and stayed back with Malen. Not that the Crone liked this. She kept trying to move away, only to have Odris keep up with her.

"We have to go along here, and then down a stair, through a belish root forest, then down a steep tunnel into the lake where the airweed grows. From there it's fairly easy to get to the Freefolk Fortress," Milla explained quietly after she had checked the next intersection.

They turned the corner, but Milla didn't keep going. Instead she stopped and frowned in thought. "Though there's bound to be an easier way — if only we can find one of the Freefolk. Perhaps we should wait a little while here. They found us easily enough before."

"I would not be sorry to rest a little," said Malen. As before, she hadn't complained. But the heat, the bad air, and the pace Milla had set had clearly taken their toll. Her golden hair, normally perfectly straight, was bedraggled and her face was flushed. Only her strange Crone's eyes were unchanged, still that deep, luminous blue.

"Rest, then," Milla said. Malen gratefully sank down, putting her back against the wall. Odris sat next to her, ignoring the Crone's angry look.

Milla didn't rest. She paced quietly back and forth, keeping an eye down both corridors while she thought about how much airweed they would need. Assuming an average of two bulbous nodules were required per person to get through the patches of bad air, a force of two thousand Icecarls would need four thousand nodules.

That was a lot of airweed to get to the far reaches of the heatways, particularly since whoever carried it would also need to use four nodules, there and back. Yet one person could probably carry twenty or thirty strands, each with six nodules. That was 120 per trip, less the four they used themselves, was 116 . . .

Milla kept calculating. She wished she had a tally stick, a flat piece of bone with holes and pegs that shipmasters and clan chiefs used in their calculations.

Leading Icecarls into battle wasn't as easy as Milla had imagined. She had always assumed it was simply a matter of leading the battle from the front, that someone else would have to think about food and supplies and all such matters.

A distant noise interrupted her calculations. Instantly she was on the alert. Malen heard it, too, and leaped up. Only Odris stayed sitting. In fact, she yawned.

Though Milla hadn't recognized the initial sound, she knew those that followed it. Footsteps. Stealthy footsteps. She could only catch them every now and then, a slight scuff or a less-than-totally-careful footfall. Someone . . . or several someones . . . were creeping along the corridor from the heat-ways.

Milla knelt down and looked around the corner, keeping low.

She saw four shapes creeping down one side of the corridor, staying as much in the shadows as they could. Milla smiled as she saw them. The leader was a tall boy with sandy hair held back with a white bone comb. He was followed by a blond girl, then a little farther back by a small boy who walked with a hesitant step. Last came a stocky, solid girl who had an oversized apron over the grimy Underfolk robe that they all wore, along with a string of airweed over her left shoulder.

All of their robes had been painted with the letter *F*.

It was Clovil, Gill, Ferek, and Inkie.

Milla kept watching them, to see if they were followed by anyone else. There was a slim chance they had been taken by the enemy, or were being forced to do Sushin's bidding.

Milla couldn't see anything following them. When they came to the hole where Milla had climbed out, they spread out around it and drew their knives. Clovil peered down quickly, then stepped back.

"No one there," he said quietly. "Guess we'd better go down farther and take a look."

Milla stepped out into the corridor.

"What for?" she asked.

All four Freefolk jumped, and Ferek let out a nervous squeak.

"You!" Clovil exclaimed.

"Milla!" Gill cried. "You didn't die!"

Gill had been the one to show Milla the way to the heatways, and they had talked quite a bit. She now looked very pleased to see the Icecarl again.

Ferek shivered and stayed silent. Inkie scowled. As far as Milla knew, Inkie never spoke at all.

Milla clapped her fists together in greeting. The Freefolk nodded or waved or did nothing, according to their natures.

"Where's Odris?" asked Gill.

"I'm here," Odris replied, drifting out behind Milla, taking a wide berth around her left hand and the Talon.

"I have another Icecarl with me, too," said Milla. "The Crone Malen."

Malen stepped out and clapped her fists. The Freefolk hadn't flinched at Odris, but they were obviously cowed by Malen. Milla tried to remember what she had told them about the Crones.

"I greet you," said Malen. "As do all the Crones of the Clans."

The Freefolk approached warily, though they did put their knives away.

"What's with the crown?" asked Clovil, pointing at the bone circlet on Milla's head. "And I thought you were going to freeze yourself to death or something, weren't you?"

"I wasn't allowed to go to the Ice," Milla replied stiffly. "It's hard to explain . . . The circlet is because I have become . . . well, it's either because I'm the Living Sword of Asteyr or the War-Chief of the Icecarls . . . I'm not sure which."

Clovil and Gill were clearly impressed by this news. Ferek looked afraid. Inkie looked the same as she ever did. Imperturbable.

"Uh, what does that mean?" asked Gill. "And why did you come back?"

"I will explain," said Milla. "But we should go to your fortress. There were Spiritshadows in the heat-way tunnels, and they may have alerted Sushin or others to our presence."

"Spiritshadows?" asked Clovil urgently. "Free ones, without Chosen? Were they with some of the Fatalists? Underfolk, I mean? We heard that two water-stirrers were forced to carry lanterns for them, and one of Ebbitt's alarms went off, so we thought they'd gone down here. In fact, when the alarm sounded again, we thought it was probably them coming back."

"They won't be coming back," said Milla. "The Spiritshadows killed them."

"Killed them!" exclaimed Gill and Clovil, as Ferek shivered even more. "But why?"

"I don't know," said Milla. "Come — we mustn't keep talking here. We must go to your fortress, and talk to Ebbitt and Crow."

The four Freefolk looked at one another.

"You haven't heard, then?" asked Gill hesitantly.

"Heard what? We've only just climbed out of the heatways!"

Gill was at a loss for words. She looked at Clovil. He opened his mouth, but didn't say anything.

Everyone got a surprise when Inkie spoke.

"Your friend Tal fought with Crow," she said in a deep and husky voice. "Crow threw his knife. Tal brought the ceiling down on him — and us — and cracked a steampipe. Ebbitt arrived just in time to make a shield of light around us all. But Crow had already been hit on the head, and the spell took a lot out of Ebbitt. They're both unconscious back at the fortress. Jarnil thinks they're going to die."

·CHAPTER· ΠΙΠΕ

The first cave Tal found was too small. The second was too wet, water dripping through it constantly. The third was just right. Long and narrow, it zigzagged into the crater wall for about fifty stretches. Tal went past the second zigzag and found a shelf of rock that would make an uncomfortable bed. But that was better than none at all, and it was far better than being discovered.

Tal sat on the shelf. The fight with the Kerfer had left him exhausted. With the weariness came a renewed sense of guilt. Sleep beckoned as a tempting refuge from remembering.

Only it wouldn't be very sensible, Tal concluded, as he fought to stay awake.

The cave kept on going, Light knew where. He didn't feel quite so confident about the crater wall being free of creatures. Not in this narrow cave, with his only avenue of escape out into the light, where he would be spotted by Sushin's minions.

He needed Adras to watch over him. But where was the Storm Shepherd? He'd been gone for quite a while. Nothing could have happened to him, or Tal would feel a lot worse than a slight ache in his stomach. Part of that ache was probably hunger, Tal suddenly thought. He hadn't eaten for ages. No wonder he was tired.

"Adras, come back," Tal whispered. He imagined himself sending out a thought to the Storm Shepherd. He pictured his thought like a small bird, flying out of the cavemouth, up into the sky, searching everywhere for a cloud that moved against the wind. "Come back, Adras, come back."

Tal concentrated on that thought for several minutes, but he had no idea if it had worked or not. He certainly didn't feel any of Adras's thoughts or feelings, as he sometimes did when the Storm Shepherd was close.

A moment later his head snapped up. He'd fallen asleep!

"I must stay awake," Tal whispered, pinching himself along his wrists. "Until Adras gets here."

Perhaps he could talk to Lokar, Tal thought. He

undid the knot in his sleeve and got out the Red Key-stone. But when he focused upon it, all he could hear was continuous mad laughter. He could see Lokar, but she did not look up from her constant pacing, and no matter what Tal said, she did not stop her crazy giggling, not even for a second. Tal put the Keystone away. He would keep himself awake.

But only a few minutes later, Tal caught himself nodding away again. Shaking his head, he slipped off the shelf and tried pacing up and down. It was even harder than swimming in the Lake of Ash. He was just so tired.

Before long he was simply staggering a few paces, turning around, and staggering back again. Each time he turned he nearly fell over.

"Come on, Adras, come on," Tal whispered again as he turned.

This time he did fall over, because as he turned, he ran straight into the cool, cloudy body of the Storm Shepherd. Judging from the fact he could hardly fit in the cave, and the healthy white puffiness of his body, Adras was clearly full of water and completely revitalized.

"I'm here!" Adras boomed. His voice was so loud that Tal felt sure that every Chosen on the lake would hear it. Hopefully they would think it was distant thunder.

"Good," said Tal sleepily. "Watch. Please. Too tired."

With that, he collapsed onto the shelf and fell straight into a sleep that was deeper than any light-dive.

Adras yawned and floated himself along next to the ledge.

"Why is it always me who has to stay awake?" he said, a little more softly than before. "When is it my turn?"

Tal woke in darkness, though sun had been leaking into the cave before he slept. For a moment he panicked, until he could raise his Sunstone and bring forth a soft, gentle light.

Adras was still floating by his side, his great cloudy chest rising and falling in a steady rhythm. Every now and again a crackle of thunder came from his nose. He was sound asleep.

Tal slipped down from the ledge and, shielding his Sunstone, crept to the cave entrance. It was night outside, but there was a crescent moon, its silver light cool and calm across the Lake of Ash.

Other lights sparkled among the houses of the Chosen Enclave and along the bridges and walkways. Like the Castle, there were many Sunstones set everywhere, stones constrained to shine only when darkness fell around them.

There was a light breeze, soft on Tal's face. He enjoyed the cool touch of it for a moment before he went back inside. He had to figure out how to get to the Empress's island, and for that, he needed to consult Lokar.

Tal felt a bit guilty as he undid the knot in his shirt and got out the Red Keystone again. He probably hadn't tried hard enough to interrupt her crazy laughing fit, which was unforgivable now that he knew how awful it was to be trapped.

"Lokar," he said, staring into the fiery depths of the Sunstone.

The Guardian of the Red Keystone still danced in a circle, her Spiritshadow eternally hopping around her. But she didn't answer Tal, at least at first. She was making a noise, though, and it wasn't the mad cackle of before. Tal focused even harder to try and hear what it was.

Singing, he realized. Lokar was singing the same song over and over again. It was a Chosen lullaby.

Sunbright stay and hold me tight
All the day's dawning, till I'm yawning
Starlight come at night, moonshine give me light
Till sun returns, till sun returns, till sun returns

Tal listened to the song twice. He'd never paid any attention to it before, but it was a pretty weird song for a Chosen of the Castle. While they enjoyed the sun in Aenir, it was a holiday place, not home. Home was covered by the Veil. Tal had never heard a Chosen say a word about missing sunshine, starshine, or moonshine. Yet there it was, in a nonsense song for children.

It had to be a very old song, predating the Veil. It was hard to remember that the Chosen of long ago had raised the Veil as a defense against Aeniran shadows. Back then, they had nowhere else to go, as travel to Aenir was forbidden. It was no wonder they sang about the sun. . . .

Lokar started singing again. Tal snapped back to the problem at hand.

"Lokar! Lokar!"

Finally the woman answered.

"What? Tal?"

"Of course it's Tal."

"How long has it been since you spoke to me?" asked Lokar. "A day, a week, a month?"

"Less than a day," replied Tal worriedly.

Lokar mumbled something to herself, then asked, "So where are we?"

Tal told her and asked her for any suggestions about how he could get to the Empress's island.

"Can't walk across the Big South Bridge," answered Lokar quickly. "No, no, no. Maybe sneak along one of the runner-ways? No. Nighttime. But where is it dark? Not on the bridges, not on the walkways, not near the houses. Where is it dark?"

"Where is it dark?" Tal repeated. "What do you mean?"

"To get across to the island unseen," Lokar explained, "you must go in darkness. All the bridges, the walkways are lit by Sunstones. How can you cross unseen?"

"Oh, no," said Tal. He could see where this was going.

"Yes," Lokar whispered. "You will have to walk across the lakebed. Under the ash."

·CHAPTER·
TEN

The Freefolk Fortress hadn't changed. Milla hadn't expected it to. Apart from the entry over the forbidding crevasse with its lava flows far below, it was a pathetic sight. Just a big cave with seven ramshackle cottages built around a central well. Even knowing that the cottages had larger, better-maintained rooms dug into the rock below them didn't impress Milla.

An old, short, and generally dried-up-looking man with razor-short gray hair was drawing water from the well, using only one hand. He looked up as Milla and the others approached, and dropped the bucket.

"That is the former Brilliance Jarnil Yannow-Kyr of the Indigo Order, once Chief Lector, is it not?"

whispered Malen to Milla. "Now self-appointed leader of the Freefolk?"

"Yes," Milla confirmed shortly. Like all the Crones, Malen had not only heard everything that had happened to Milla but had walked through her mind and seen a lot of her memories as well.

Jarnil didn't seem overly pleased to see Milla again, particularly in company with another Icecarl. But he did come to greet them. Milla noticed that he now wore a Sunstone openly, on a gold chain around his neck. She hadn't seen it before. It was a large stone, about as big as a baby's fist, and shone with an indigo light.

"Milla of the Far-Raiders," Jarnil said, formally bowing and giving the briefest flash of light from his Sunstone. "To what do we owe the honor of your return?"

"I have come for airweed," said Milla bluntly. "I want to enlist the Freefolk to help me deliver it through the heatways."

"What!" croaked Jarnil, his face losing all its color. His bad arm twitched and quivered. "Airweed? What for?"

It was Malen who answered him. She strode forward and gripped his shaking hand.

"Long ago, our peoples joined together to defeat

the creatures of Aenir. To prevent them coming as shadows here, we raised the Veil and cast the Forgetting in Aenir. But your Chosen did not keep the pact of long ago. You have been to Aenir and brought back shadows. Now the creatures of Aenir have broken the Forgetting and seek to break the Veil. They must be stopped. As the Chosen have fallen into error, it lies upon the Clans to do what must be done."

"Who are you?" whispered Jarnil. He couldn't stop himself from looking into the Crone's deep, luminous eyes. "What are you doing to my arm?"

"I am Malen, daughter of Arla, daughter of Halla, daughter of Luen, daughter of Rucia, daughter of Nuthe, in the line of Grettir since the Ruin of the Ship. Your arm has been twisted in your mind. I am untwisting it."

Milla suppressed a gasp as she heard Malen's full lineage. No wonder she had not been fully introduced to her before. It was a Crone's privilege to speak her full name or not, and Crone Mothers were simply known by their titles. Even so, Milla wished she had known before. Malen was the daughter of Arla, the Shield Mother who Milla had fought and killed in her desperate rush to the Ruin Ship to warn the Crones.

"Let me go!" Jarnil protested. He was almost weeping. Whatever Malen was doing, it obviously hurt a lot. The Freefolk by Milla's side shifted nervously, but didn't do anything.

Finally Malen let go. Jarnil slumped at her feet. But when he pressed his hands against the floor to get up, both arms moved normally. Jarnil stood and stared down at his open palms, flexing his fingers and rotating his wrists.

"I . . . I thank you," he mumbled. "Yet, I cannot . . . cannot condone what you intend. It is not right that the Castle . . . I will forbid the Freefolk to gather airweed. There, I have said it. You will get no airweed!"

Only Milla listened to him. The Freefolk were all staring at Malen.

"That was great!" said Clovil.

"Do you think you can make Crow better?" asked Gill. "And Ebbitt?"

"Bennem," said Inkie, surprising everyone again. "Make Bennem better."

Bennem was Crow's older brother. He had been twice in the Hall of Nightmares, and was now lost in dream.

"Let us see," replied Malen. "Take me to them."

"No airweed," Jarnil repeated. His usually smooth voice broke.

"The world is changing," said Milla. "You cannot hold a Selski. You can only kill it or get out of the way. Even if you kill it you must still get out of the way."

"I don't understand," muttered Jarnil.

"We will get airweed," said Milla. "Icecarls will come. I will make sure you are not harmed."

Jarnil sighed and, with an effort, drew himself up to his full height — a head short of Milla. He bowed again, this time both his arms moving gracefully into the perfect position. He did not give light from his Sunstone.

"Do what you must," he said and turned away.

"Do not leave this place," Milla instructed.

Jarnil didn't answer, but he left the bridge and went into his own cottage, gently shutting the door behind him.

Milla watched him go and wondered if she should have killed him. Somehow she didn't feel like it, even though he was undoubtedly planning something against her and the Icecarls.

Nothing was as easy as she had once imagined. She had always thought that when you saw an enemy, or thought someone might be one, you killed them.

But when it came down to it, Milla remembered very few actual killings of people among the Clans, because there were few real enemies. There were plenty of fights, and plenty of blood was shed, but it rarely ended in a death. The deaths that did occur were always in the heat of battle. There seemed something basically wrong about killing a little old man who was more like a Crone than any sort of fighting Icecarl.

Perhaps Jarnil would attack her, Milla thought, so she could kill him without having to think about it.

She shook her head at this notion and strode off to the cottage where the others had gone. If Malen — *Daughter of Arla* echoed in her head — could help Crow and Ebbitt, they might be able to tell her what had happened to Tal. She did not believe that he had been killed by Crow. Milla was bound to Tal, after a fashion, by Icecarl oaths as well as the magic they had experienced together. She thought she would know if he was dead.

Odris followed her at a safe distance, always keeping to the right, away from the Talon.

·CHAPTER·
ELEVEΠ

"I can't walk across the lakebed!" exclaimed Tal. "I'll be eaten in a minute!"

"There is a way," replied Lokar. "It is fortunate you have a Storm Shepherd on hand. First, you will have to make a suit of Chromatic armor. Make it a hand-width too large in all ways, so the Storm Shepherd can cram in with you."

"Chromatic armor?" asked Tal. "What's that?"

"Don't the Lectors teach anything anymore?" grumbled Lokar. "It's armor made of light, of course. In this case you have to make sure it's airtight."

"But how do I make it?" asked Tal. He couldn't help but be fascinated by the idea. "And how do I breathe?"

"The Storm Shepherd," said Lokar. She paused

then, as it was clear Tal didn't get the idea, she continued, "He's made mostly of concentrated air and water vapor."

Tal wrinkled his nose.

"So I'll be breathing Adras?" he asked. "That sounds disgusting."

"You won't even notice," said Lokar. "Nor will he, as long as you don't stay in the armor for more than a few hours."

Tal considered this. It was pretty revolting, but it did seem the only way he could cross the lakebed. Then another nasty thought struck him. He remembered the Kerfer being sucked straight under.

"So I'll be in armor," he said. "But what if something swallows me whole?"

"Chromatic armor can be fashioned to radiate intense heat. You'll be comfortable inside, but to anything outside you'll feel like a red-hot belish root. Nothing will want to eat you, I promise."

"I'd better ask Adras," Tal said. The Storm Shepherd was still snoring in midair. Tal prodded him in the arm. Nothing happened, so he punched him lightly, his fist sinking into the cloudy shoulder.

"What!" boomed Adras, sitting up with a start. "I'm awake! I didn't fall asleep."

"Yes you did. But that doesn't matter since we

seem to have survived. Now, how do you feel about crossing the bottom of the lake inside armor made of light while I use your air to breathe?"

"What?" asked Adras again. He shook his head and cleaned out one huge ear with a puffy finger. "What did you say?"

Tal explained. Three times. He explained they couldn't fly because they'd be seen. Adras's main problem with the plan was going under the ash. He didn't like the idea of that at all.

When Adras finally agreed to give it a try, Tal looked back into the Red Keystone.

Lokar was sighing again.

"How long have you been gone?" asked the Guardian.

"Only fifteen minutes, at the most."

"Fifteen minutes . . ." Lokar shook her head. "Gone with the hours, gone with the days. Listen, Tal. I will explain how to make a suit of Chromatic armor. Are you familiar with Indigo crafting and Blue welds?"

Tal had to admit that he was not.

"Violet bonds? Yellow crimping? Red shifts? Orange weaves?"

Only the last two were familiar to Tal. He said so, and Lokar sighed again.

"Then I will begin with the basics. Listen carefully. We will take it in stages. I will explain, then you will do what I have taught you, then we will go on to the next step."

For the next six hours, Tal labored under Lokar's directions. He made several false starts, and was continually having to begin again. But slowly the suit of Chromatic armor began to build in the cave. It looked like a man-shaped sarcophagus made of rainbows, all seven colors swirling through it. It was fashioned in two parts that hinged down one side, so Tal could get in and close it on himself.

Finally, the Chromatic armor was ready. It lay glowing on the floor, colors constantly chasing and mixing across its surface. It looked solid and heavy, but Tal had no trouble standing it up and opening it a bit more so it stood upright on its own.

"How do I see out of it?" he asked Lokar. As far as he could tell the suit was all rainbow light, with no transparent parts, even in the helmet.

"You will be able to see from inside when the suit is closed," replied Lokar. "Provided you've made it correctly. It is particularly important that the unraveling cord is in the right place on the outside."

Tal looked at the suit. Sure enough, there among the moving rainbows in the middle of the chest plate was a solid circle of violet light. When it was time to open the suit, he would grasp that and pull it, springing the suit open. The unraveling cord was essential. Tal remembered the near disaster he'd had creating the minor veil, trapping Adras in its making, and almost asphyxiating himself and Crow.

"I guess we'd better go, then," he said. "I'll talk to you as soon as I can, Lokar."

Lokar didn't answer. She was singing the song again. Tal looked away, breaking contact. He tied the Red Keystone into his shirt once more, for safe-keeping.

"Time for us to get in," Tal announced to Adras, who had been floating near the ceiling. The Storm Shepherd grumbled a low thunderous rumble, but lowered his legs to the floor.

Tal opened up the two halves of the suit a bit more, then stepped back into it, shuffling his feet into position and setting his shoulders in place. The suit, as instructed, was too large. When it was closed there would be a good handspan between Tal and the sides.

Adras drifted over and stared at him.

"Where am I supposed to go?"

Tal hadn't thought about how they would actually get in. After a moment's reflection, he stepped out.

"You get in first, and then I'll squeeze in against you," he said.

"It's pretty small," Adras objected.

He started to go in face first, until Tal stopped him and made him back in. Though Adras was much bigger to start with, he compressed well into the armor. His cloud body could shrink and expand enormously.

"Shrink a bit more," Tal instructed, as he backed in himself. "We have to both fit."

"I don't like this," said Adras. "It's a prison."

"No it isn't!" exclaimed Tal. "It's only for a few hours. There!"

He was in. It was weird being pressed up against the Storm Shepherd. He felt like a clammy sponge. Tal hoped Lokar was right about Tal being able to breathe some of the air that Adras was made out of.

He reached forward and grabbed a thin blue circle that had held constant among the rainbows of the other half of the armor. He pulled it and it came apart in his hand, breaking into a thousand tiny motes of blue light.

"Dark take it!" cursed Tal. He thought he'd broken it. Then the suit of armor started to close. Tal quickly pulled his arm back into position and kept absolutely still. Adras squirmed a bit around him.

"Stay still!"

Slowly the other half of the suit closed in on Tal. He watched it inexorably shutting and had a moment of panic. What if he'd made it wrong, and the suit crushed him? What if he couldn't breathe? What if Adras had too much water vapor in him and not enough air and they ran out halfway?

The suit closed. Rainbows danced across Tal's face. He took several deep breaths, and was relieved that there seemed to be something to breathe.

Slowly the rainbows in front of his face faded. He could see out into the cave, though flashes of red and blue did keep crossing his vision.

Experimentally, Tal raised one arm. It moved easily enough. Tal could see his armored limb rising, rainbows coruscating all over. But as he raised his arm higher, it got harder to move, until it was stuck and no matter how he strained it would not move at all.

He tried to move his other arm. It went a few inches and then froze, too.

Fear hit Tal again. He'd made the armor incorrectly and now he couldn't even reach the unraveling cord.

They were stuck in here forever!

·CHAPTER· TWELVE

Ebbitt and Crow were in one of the cellar rooms, lying in beds arranged directly under the single weak Sunstone in the ceiling. Crow's head was heavily bandaged. Ebbitt looked uninjured, but he was unconscious, too. His great cat Spiritshadow lay across the end of the bed. It raised its head as Milla and Odris entered, but didn't get up.

Malen was already examining Bennem. The big man sat quietly on a stool at the end of Crow's bed. The Crone was staring him in the eye, with one hand on his forehead. Gill, Clovil, Ferek, and Inkie were all ranged alongside Crow's bed, watching the Crone intently.

Malen withdrew her hand. Bennem smiled and turned back to look at Crow.

"He is gone too deep," said Malen. "I think that

he might be brought back, but I do not have the skill for it. Perhaps when one of the Crone Mothers comes, or one of the others who knows more healing than I do."

"What about Crow?" asked Milla. She wanted to talk to him about Tal, and also to ask his advice about attacking the Castle. Crow had spent many years making plans to defeat the Chosen. He would have useful knowledge.

"I haven't looked at him yet," said Malen. She walked to the head of Crow's bed and bent down to listen to his chest. Then she took the pulse at his neck and lifted one eyelid. The other Freefolk continued to follow her every move, obviously fascinated.

"Who bandaged him?" she asked. "I need to remove it."

"Jarnil," said Gill. "He knows the most healing. He did light magic on the cuts on Crow's head, and that stopped the bleeding. But he hasn't woken up."

Malen nodded thoughtfully. She started to unwind the bandage, but stopped as Bennem got up from his stool, obviously distressed at what she was doing to his brother.

"I need to see," Malen said to him. She looked him in the eye and repeated her words. Whether he understood them or not, Bennem was calmed, and sat back down.

Malen undid the last of the bandages, revealing a nasty, puckered, and very new scar across the top of Crow's forehead. It was partially healed, but looked red and inflamed. Milla had seen wounds like that before. Usually people died of them, if the Crones didn't arrive in time.

Malen peered closely at the cut. Milla looked, too. She knew some healing light magic, but she didn't mention it. A head wound was a Crone's business, not for someone with only a basic understanding of Sunstone healing.

"I will need to clean and treat this," Malen said. "I have some of the medicines I need with me, but I will require boiled water and kriggi."

"Boiled water's easy," replied Clovil. "What are kriggi?"

"Ah, little white grubs that eat meat," replied Malen. "Do you know of them?"

"Maggots," said a voice from the next bed. "Twisty little beggars. Try the composting tunnels at the southern end of Underfolk Five."

Everyone looked across. It was Ebbitt who had spoken. Everyone but Malen knew his voice. But he still lay there, apparently asleep.

"Ebbitt," said Milla.

One of Ebbitt's eyes opened a fraction. The pupil moved until it was looking straight at Milla.

"Nice crown," said Ebbitt. "Interesting fingernail. Where did you get that?"

"The heatways," said Milla. "The same skeleton that had the Sunstone you split for Tal and me. Are you all right?"

"Weary," said Ebbitt. He shut his eye and opened the other one. "Stonkered. Worn out. Too old for emergency light magic."

"You saved us, though," said Clovil. "We are grateful."

Ebbitt gave a tiny shrug.

"Couldn't stand the thought of the mess," he said. "Besides, Tal didn't mean it. Accident."

"Inkie told me that Crow threw his knife at Tal," said Milla. "Do you know what happened to him?"

"Knife missed," said Ebbitt. "Should have had a fork as well. Maybe a spoon. Whole set."

Milla was used to Ebbitt and his *unique* way of talking. She continued her questions.

"Do you know where Tal is now? Odris says Adras has gone back to Aenir. Could Tal have gone, too?"

"Maybe," said Ebbitt. "He had the Red Keystone.

Should have brought it to me. Then again, he probably thinks I got squashed. Who knows where the caveroach goes? Ask Crow when your charming companion has opened his head. Should use healing magic but too tired. Get Lokar to do it properly this time. Anyone seen the Codex?"

Everyone shook their heads. Malen looked at Milla, obviously thinking that the old man was sick and raving. Milla whispered that Ebbitt was always like that.

"I have," added Ebbitt. Then he rolled over, closed both eyes firmly, and refused to answer anyone else's questions.

Gill went to get hot water while Malen removed a small case of Wreska hide from under her light furs. She unfolded it on the bed, revealing lots of tiny pockets filled with medicines made from seaweed and the many beasts of the Ice. Milla only recognized a few of them, like the powdered Merwin horn, still faintly glowing, and a vial of very rare Ursek tears.

While the healing preparations were under way, Milla explained to Clovil her plan to enlist the Freefolk to transport airweed to the halfway point in the heatway tunnels. Clovil listened intently, but wouldn't commit himself or any friendly Freefolk or Underfolk until they could talk to Crow about it. Milla wanted him to make a decision without Crow.

"We need to move quickly," Milla urged. "Right now all the Chosen are in Aenir, their bodies sleeping above us. If I can bring enough Icecarls equipped with shadowbags and other such weapons into the Castle, we can capture or destroy the Spiritshadows that guard them before the Chosen can come back from Aenir. A surprise attack will mean there is less damage to the Castle — and fewer people will die, including Underfolk. Just think what a full-scale battle will mean to your people, even if they're trying to stay out of the way."

"And when we have won," she added, "your help will ensure that all Underfolk are treated properly. Icecarls are always faithful to sworn allies."

"Crow is the leader," Clovil answered uncomfortably.

"I think . . . I think . . . we should help Milla," said Ferek. He glanced anxiously at Crow. "The Icecarls will come anyway. Best we be friends from the start."

"What's that?" Gill asked, as she staggered back in with a huge crystal tub of hot water, her face red from the steam rolling off it and the effort. She put the water down next to the bed.

"I found some old biscuits, too," she added, taking a handful out of her pocket to put on the bed. A whole lot of maggots fell out onto the blanket. "Are those kriggi?"

Malen nodded and herded the squirming maggots into a neat pile, ready for use. Then she dropped some medicines into the pot of steaming water and stirred it with her knife. When the blade came out it was bright purple.

Everyone except Milla looked the other way as the Crone began to cut.

After a few seconds of strained silence as everyone tried not to hear the Crone at work, Clovil explained to Gill what they were discussing.

"We might as well get started right away," said Gill. She didn't seem to think there was any difficulty in joining forces with the Icecarls. "There's no point in waiting for Crow, Clovil. He won't be better for ages. I'm sure we can get Korvim to come back for this, and he'll bring others!"

"It's a big decision," warned Clovil.

"Of course it is," said Gill. "But haven't we been waiting all this time to do something big? This is it! This is our chance! Everything is going to be different. No more Chosen lording it over us. No more Hall of Nightmares! Freedom for our people!"

"I hope so," said Clovil. He looked at Milla. "Perhaps we will just be exchanging one lot of rulers for another."

"You are free to choose now," said Milla. "I promise you we will help you decide your own fate in the future."

Clovil looked into her eyes. Whatever he saw there made up his mind.

"We'll get the airweed. Tell us where it has to be taken."

"Good," said Milla. "I will draw you a map. When Malen is finished with Crow, she will tell the Crones to expect you, and to prepare for the assault!"

·CHAPTER·
THIRTEEN

"Adras!" yelled Tal. "We're stuck!"

"Don't shout," grumbled Adras. His voice was incredibly loud, right at Tal's ear. "Do you mean I don't have to stay still?"

Tal's arms suddenly spread wide and his legs shuffled forward. The suit toppled. Reflexively, Tal tried to put his hands down to break the fall, but his arms were wrenched the other way.

They bounced once, got halfway up, then Tal found his knees bending and his arms windmilling. Finally he realized what was happening. Adras had stopped Tal moving before, and now the Storm Shepherd's movements were directing the armor. Tal was so much weaker that he was just a passenger inside the suit.

"Adras!" he ordered. "Stay still for a moment. We have to work together."

Adras obeyed and the suit slowly settled down.

"Right. Adras, please follow my motions, but don't use too much strength or overdo it. I'm going to raise my left arm now."

He started to raise his arm, felt Adras join in, and then the limb was jerking all over the place.

"Ow! Ow! Easy!" exclaimed Tal. "Now the right arm."

It took quite a lot of practice, but eventually they managed to work out how to move inside the suit. Tal moved first, then Adras would join in, using only a fraction of his strength.

Tal was glad no one could see them as they jerked about the cave, occasionally crashing into the walls and falling down. Even when they'd worked it out, their movements were still stiff and clumsy.

They headed out of the cave. Tal wanted to stop near the entrance and have a look around, but mistimed stopping, so they staggered out and tipped over. While they got up, Tal cursed and Adras complained, until the Chosen boy suddenly realized that he didn't know if sound traveled outside the armor or not.

That shut them both up. Fortunately, they didn't

seem to have attracted any attention. At least not with the noise. Tal was further alarmed to see just how bright the suit was out in the night. Not as bright as a Sunstone, but the rainbow surface did glow, even before he started the defensive spells that would make it burn red-hot.

They needed to get under the ash quickly. Tal started for the lake and quickly waded in. He had a moment's worry as the ash closed over his head, but the suit was airtight. Or at least ash-tight.

Even though the ash was mixed with clear crystal, it was still very hard to see more than a few stretches through it. Tal took a few steps down the steeply shelving lakebed before he thought about another problem.

Without knowing where he was going, he could easily get lost or turned around. How was he going to find the Empress's island?

He thought of Milla then, and her unerring sense of direction on the Ice. What would Milla do if she were here?

Follow a bridge, came the answer.

Tal smiled as he thought of Milla telling him what to do, but the smile faded as he recalled that she was probably dead, too, gone to the Ice. Someone else who was dead because of his actions.

He was alone.

"Stop it," mumbled Adras.

"What?"

"That feeling in your head, when it gets all heavy and your heart aches," replied Adras. "It makes me sick."

Tal didn't answer. Instead he started moving along the lakeshore, keeping his helmet just a fraction out of the ash. The Big South Bridge — one of the main bridges to the central cluster of Chosen houses — was about eight hundred stretches away. He would follow the shoreline to it, then follow the bridge's foundations out.

As he got closer to the bridge and its steady Sunstone light, Tal went deeper into the ash to avoid detection.

He was surprised to find as he went deeper that the lakebed was not smooth as he'd imagined. It was often broken up, and there were deep holes and crevasses. He had to pick his way carefully and several times he almost fell into what might be a very deep pit. The biggest problem was that he only ever saw them at the last second, because the visibility was so bad.

At least that was the biggest immediate problem. Tal couldn't help remembering the sudden disappearance of the stunned Kerfer. Something really big and really hungry was down here in the ash. He really, really hoped it wasn't looking for dessert after its Kerfer dinner.

It took what seemed like hours before he reached the Big South Bridge. In fact, he almost walked straight under it and continued on, but he ran into some cut squares of stone. That made him turn back to shallower waters, carefully poke his head out, and check his position.

He was under the bridge. Sunstone light shone down to either side. He could certainly hear through the suit, he discovered, because there were heavy footsteps above, and the sound of voices. Tal tried to hear what they were saying, but they were too far above. All the bridges and the houses stood at least forty stretches above the lake, probably to ensure the Chosen's safety from things with long tentacles.

Tal strode back down the sloping lakebed in what he hoped was the same direction as the bridge. It was, as discovered before long when he almost walked straight into a pylon, built of massive blocks of shaped stone. It was hard to tell in the constantly changing light from the suit, but to Tal it looked like the stone was a dark green — not volcanic gray or black — which meant it had been quarried some-where else and brought to the crater.

Tal slowly worked his way around to the other side of the pylon. He was about to launch off deeper into the lake in the hope that the next pylon wouldn't be far away when he saw a faint glow off to his right. A soft violet light, diffused by the ash.

He hesitated for a moment, then decided to in-vestigate. Just in case, he kept one finger on the red loop on his chest, the one that would make the suit super-hot on the outside — and only on the out-side. He hoped.

When he got closer, Tal saw that the light came from a cluster of Sunstones. They were grouped at the top of a long pole that was thrust deep into the lakebed. Tal lumbered closer still, and saw that it wasn't a pole. It was actually a giant harpoon, made from Chosen crystal, one of the few materials that was identical in both the Dark World and Aenir. There were Sunstones all along the shaft, though most were long extinguished. Only the cluster at the end of the harpoon and some Sunstones on the part of the point that was exposed were still shining.

"Weird," said Tal. Why was a giant harpoon stuck in the lakebed?

"How long do we have to stay in here?" Adras

asked plaintively. "I want to fly. I need to see the sky."

"Soon," soothed Tal. The harpoon was an interesting mystery, but Adras was right. They shouldn't be wasting time. He turned away from it and started walking.

Fortunately the Chosen who had built the bridge had also smoothed the lakebed underneath it. Tal discovered that this helped his navigation a lot. Whenever he encountered tumbled stones or broken ground, he worked back to where the lakebed was undisturbed.

Even on the smoother ground it was hard going. Adras tried to cooperate, but they had both reached the limits of their dexterity in the suit, and still rolled, lumbered, and tripped up. Their Chromatic armor walking would make a great show for Chosen children, Tal thought as they got their legs unsynchronized and came to a sudden, swaying halt.

As they got going again, Tal saw another glow ahead. It looked the same as the one he'd seen a hundred stretches back. Had they gotten turned around somehow?

He headed up to it, and for a few seconds was convinced that they had ended up back where they'd been. There was another harpoon, glowing with Sunstones.

But, Tal noticed, this harpoon had different patterns. It was another one, so at least they hadn't turned around.

This time he went right up to the harpoon and gingerly touched the crystal. It didn't move at all, even when he pushed quite hard. He was about to withdraw his hand when Adras suddenly decided to help, shifting his cloud-flesh around to the front of Tal and exerting his full strength.

The harpoon shifted very slightly. Instantly the remaining Sunstones on it flashed brightly and Tal felt a vibration run through the lakebed and up through his boots.

"Stop!" he shouted. He pulled his hand back, but it just bounced on the inside of the glove. Adras did stop, but not for a second or two. In that short time, the harpoon shifted a finger-width, and the Sunstones flashed again.

This time the vibration through the lakebed was strong enough to shake Tal's teeth. He looked down and saw faint cracks running through the stone around the harpoon's point.

"We'd better leave this alone," Tal said. Whatever the harpoons were part of, it was serious magic and he had been stupid to interfere with it.

"You don't want me to pull it out?" asked Adras. Tal had the unpleasant sight of the Storm Shepherd's eyeball floating under his chin so Adras could take a look. "It could be useful. We could stick Sushin with it, like Milla did."

"No," replied Tal hastily. "Come on."

They backed away, almost falling over, then took a wide circle around the harpoon. As Tal had half expected, there was another pylon just beyond the harpoon. He went around it and when he saw a familiar glow on the other side, didn't go and investigate.

"Concentrate on the task," Tal whispered to himself as he successfully put one foot in front of another.

"What?" asked Adras. The Storm Shepherd apparently couldn't walk and talk at the same time, because the next step stalled as Tal moved his leg forward and Adras didn't. They only managed to recover by taking a series of tiny, hopping steps that Tal knew looked particularly stupid.

"What did you say?" Adras asked again.

Tal took a deep breath. Adras wasn't the only one who wanted out of the suit.

"I didn't say anything to you," Tal said, as calmly as he could. "I was talking to myself."

Adras snorted, nearly blowing Tal's eardrums in.

"How much farther is it?"

"I don't know!"

Adras didn't talk after that for quite a long time, as they found and went around two more pylons. Unfortunately it wasn't a companionable silence. It was a sulky semi-silence punctuated by snorts and long-suffering sighs. Adras also kept his eyeballs floating around at the edge of Tal's vision, just in front of the boy's ears, though he could see perfectly well if he left them on Tal's shoulders.

Tal was thinking they should hit the sixth pylon soon when Adras spoke again.

"What's that?"

"I don't know!"

Tal answered automatically, before he even saw what Adras was referring to. When he did see it, his hand went instantly to the red loop and pulled it.

For once, Adras cooperated perfectly. Unfortunately they should have stopped first. Their last, fateful step had carried them straight into the thing Adras had spotted a second before.

A wall of white scales, higher than Tal, stretched as far as he could see to the left and right.

As they touched it, the scaly flesh rippled, but the thing didn't move. Tal looked up and along, his heart hammering in his chest. It was some sort of worm or snake-thing, but far larger than it had a right to be. As far as he could tell, it was actually wrapped around the next pylon.

The scales rippled again. The worm flexed a little and the section in front of Tal slid along a few stretches, sending waves through the ash.

"The head must be that way," Tal whispered. He didn't know why he was whispering.

He started moving the other way, but as he moved, the worm moved, too. It seemed to be irritated, the huge body rippling sideways as well as moving forward.

Tal looked down at the front of the suit. It was no longer rainbow-colored, but a deep red that was verging into black. Tal felt no difference, but the armor was clearly working as Lokar had promised. It was turning red-hot.

It was turning red-hot while they were right next to a gigantic worm, which at any moment could get annoyed and sweep its body across and turn Tal and Adras, armored or not, into pulp.

"Back up," Tal said urgently as the worm got more and more agitated. It was sliding back and forth and rolling its body, the scales lifting as if it sought to cool itself underneath.

The worm rolled again, its vast body crashing down right where Tal had been a moment before.

"Back, faster!" shrieked Tal. He was windmilling his arms to stay upright as they staggered back. If they fell now, it would be all over.

Then they hit something else. Tal tried to turn left and Adras tried to turn right. Adras won, but the suit spun out of control, pitching them to the lakebed.

They landed face-up. Tal stared as the worm rolled closer and closer. Then he looked to see what they'd run into.

He caught the briefest glimpse of a cavernous, bony mouth big enough to snap up a dozen suits of armor.

Then it closed over him.

·CHAPTER·
FOURTEEN

Whatever had swooped in and eaten them accelerated away so swiftly that Tal momentarily blacked out. Then he started to struggle, punching wildly and kicking, until Adras joined in to help and made it too difficult.

In his initial panic, Tal hadn't looked around. Now he saw that they were still in the creature's mouth. Whatever it was didn't seem bothered by the heat, possibly because the armor was totally surrounded by ash swallowed at the same time.

Tal tried to sit up, but fell over as their swallower suddenly tilted one way and then the other. It felt like it was still moving very quickly, though it was hard to tell from inside.

"At least it hasn't swallowed," Tal said after a while. It was still impossible to sit up. They'd twice

flipped over completely and if he hadn't been cushioned by Adras, Tal would have been seriously
bruised inside the armor.

"I want to get out," replied Adras. "Out of the
monster, out of the armor, out!"

"So do I!" said Tal.

He thought furiously. What was the story Milla
had told him? About Ulla Strong-Arm when she
was swallowed by a broken-jawed Selski? She'd cut
herself out of the Selski's stomach. But he didn't
have a sword. Maybe he could burn his way out . . .

Tal started swimming through the ash to reach
the side or the floor of the creature's mouth. But
every time he got close there was nothing to hang
on to and the next sudden swerve or turn threw him
back where he started, suspended in the middle.

Then Tal saw two protruding bulbs of flesh at the
rear of the mouth. They were about as big as he
was. Though they were constantly quivering, he
could at least try and hold on to them.

They weren't tonsils, but Tal thought they might
be the monster's equivalent. If he could tickle them,
or annoy them, or burn them, the monster might
throw up.

"Let's grab whatever they are and see what hap-
pens!" he said, and pointed. A moment later he was

hurled across the mouth by a sudden zigzag, but Adras got the message. Together they struggled to swim across to the fleshy appendages.

It was a case of two strokes forward and one fall back, but finally they were close enough. Tal hesitated. For a fleeting moment he wondered if it could get any worse. Then he embraced the closer appendage with his now black-hot arms.

It wriggled and shook as Tal held it, but the exposed gray-blue flesh didn't seem to burn. He gripped it tighter and tried to throw himself backward and forward. But it was like holding on to a tree trunk in a gale. It went wherever it wanted to and Tal only just managed to hang on.

Then the mouth opened a fraction and a fresh current of ash swept through the mouth. Tal shouted in triumph, and prepared to let go so they could get vomited out.

But the monster didn't vomit. The mouth snapped open wide and a huge wave of ash came crashing in. Tal was picked up and hurled past the tonsil-things and down a tunnel that was all too gulletlike. Halfway along, the suit was gripped by a tremendous suction and fired like a spitball down a tube. Tal and Adras were twisted and turned and spun about so Tal could hardly see where they were.

They exploded out into a large chamber that Tal guessed was the creature's stomach. It was only half full of ash and crystal, and besides Tal and Adras in the armor, there were several things floating on the surface. Things that had obviously once enjoyed some sort of life in the lake.

Two long gray tendrils came out of the stomach wall, reached down, and picked up a big chunk of what looked like a Kerfer. The tendrils held it above the ash while another thicker tendril moved across it, coating it with a sticky yellow substance. Then the first two tendrils shoved the Kerfer tidbit hard against the stomach wall. A tiny hole there expanded to admit the chunk. The tendrils pushed it in and the hole snapped shut.

"I feel sick," said Tal.

The tendrils swooped back down. They almost touched Tal, but recoiled at the last moment. The third tendril hovered close, but it didn't touch the suit, or spew forth any of the yellow mucus.

Then the suction started again. Ash rose up all around Tal and Adras, almost pure ash without the crystals that made it more see-through. The ash coated the suit's helmet so they couldn't see at all.

A second later Tal was slammed down one end of the suit as it was gripped in a mighty suction. The suction increased. The suit was being buffeted and Tal shook around like a pea in a pod as they accelerated. There was an explosion that deafened Tal and rattled his teeth and they spun end over end before coming to a crashing halt that would probably have killed Tal if Adras hadn't spread around him and cushioned the blow.

After a few seconds of wondering what in the name of Light had just happened, Tal wiped the front of the helmet, to clear the ash. After a few wipes, he had it clear enough to see that they had collided with a huge block of stone.

They were out of the monster, free and clear in the lake. Tal closed his eyes and breathed a sigh of relief. It wasn't how Ulla Strong-Arm would have done it, and it wasn't the stuff of legend. But he didn't care.

He looked up at the stone. It was smaller than the bridge pylons, but it was shaped stone and it went straight up. It was probably the foundation of a Chosen house.

"Let's climb up and see where we are," he said to Adras. "The sooner we get out of this lake, the better."

It was a long climb. Evidently the creature that had swallowed them was a denizen of the deepest part of the lake.

It was a nervous climb, too. Tal found that it took all his willpower to concentrate on the climb and not look over his shoulder every few minutes. He kept expecting to see the shadow of those giant jaws. What if the thing decided to keep them next time?

By the time they reached the top, Tal had almost decided not to go back under again. Whatever the risks of detection, they would leave the suit and sneak along a bridge. Then he would steal a boat to get to the Empress's island. He couldn't face being eaten and . . . *ejected* . . . by a monster again.

But when they got to the top of the stone, Tal discovered that it didn't join a bridge or a house. It just stopped, about half his height below the surface.

Tal crouched on top of the stone and looked around. It was still night, which was good. Without having his Sunstone accessible to check the time, he had feared it would be past dawn already. The moon had risen, though, and it was two-thirds full and far too bright for comfort.

It took him a while to get his bearings. They had been brought by the monster to the other side of the lake, the less inhabited side. There was the main cluster of Chosen homes off in the distance, and the Big South Bridge. There was the East Bridge, and the Orange Common House he knew well.

And there, no more than two hundred stretches away, was the dark shape of the Empress's island. He could only see the bright pools of light from a few Sunstones on it, most on the far side closer to the main part of the Enclave. There were no lights at all on the lakeshore facing Tal.

Tal looked at it carefully. There was a time when he would have just headed for it straight away. He was more thoughtful now. Why was the island and the closer shore the only place that wasn't lit up? How was it defended against all the creatures that could crawl up its shores out of the lake?

"Out," said Adras, cutting into Tal's thoughts.

"Soon, very soon," said Tal. He thought for a moment longer. There was no way he was going to climb back down and walk across the lakebed to the island. They would have to take a chance, even with the moon shining so brightly.

"Adras. Are you strong enough to fly us both to the island?"

"Yes," Adras confirmed instantly. Tal worried about that for a moment, since he knew Adras would say anything to get out.

"All right. I'm going to open the armor. As soon as I step out, I want you to pick me up and fly me just to the edge of the island. To the edge. Got that?"

Adras nodded, pushing Tal's head forward so sharply he nearly cricked his neck.

Tal grabbed the violet loop and pulled it, before Adras could nod again.

·CHAPTER·
FIFTEEN

The suit of armor didn't open. It blew apart. Thousands of red-hot shards flew in all directions, falling into the lake like strange hail. One fell near Tal's foot. He could feel the heat from it, even through the ash and crystal.

Adras didn't spring up into the air as Tal had planned. He stayed where he was, until the last flaming fragment of the armor fell to earth.

"Lokar didn't tell me it would do that," croaked Tal. His mouth had gotten suddenly dry. "What if I'd been standing next to someone?"

"They'd be very cross," replied Adras. He was slowly billowing out to his full size.

"I hope no one . . . nothing noticed." Tal looked around. The surface of the lake was still and there was no sign of any activity off in the lit-up areas.

Adras launched out of the ash and floated above Tal's head. He didn't look any the worse for having supplied breathing air for several hours, or for being compressed in the suit of armor. But he was clearly much happier to be out.

Tal held up his arms and winced even before Adras grabbed him. For some reason the Storm Shepherd knew only one shoulder-dislocating technique for picking Tal up.

Cloudy hands met around Tal's wrists and the expected savage jerk came. For a few seconds Tal's legs trailed in the ash, bringing unpleasant images of fishing expeditions and brightly colored lures. Then Adras rose higher and Tal came free.

"Don't get too high," cautioned Tal as they rose up to forty or fifty stretches above the lake. The moon was bright, bright enough to cast a shadow from the flying Storm Shepherd and the Chosen boy dangling beneath him. Tal watched the shadow flicker across the lake. It was strange to think that here in Aenir, shadows were only ever dark reflections and nothing more.

The Empress's island looked peaceful enough by moonlight. Looking down at it, Tal could see that most of the place was taken up by carefully ordered gardens. There were statues spread among the gardens, and several pools of what must be real water, silver in the moonlight. Off on the southern side there was an L-shaped house, its windows mostly dark. It was roofed with crystal tiles that had to be sprinkled with Sunstones, for they twinkled in different colors rather than reflecting the moonlight. In front of the house there was a courtyard covered by a canopy of crystal leaves. There were Sunstones shining brightly under that canopy, but Tal couldn't see what they illuminated.

It all looked very pretty and comfortable. But there must also be guards of some sort, Tal thought. He would have to evade them, and somehow get enough time to tell the Empress of the danger Sushin presented, of the threat to the Veil and the whole Dark World.

Adras glided down as instructed and set Tal down on the very edge of the island. The landing was as gentle as could be expected, which meant that Tal fell over. He was surprised to find that he had landed on soft grass. As he got up he saw that it grew right up to the lakeshore and the ash. No normal grass would do that. It felt normal enough, though, just like the lawns in the garden caverns of the Castle.

There was a path not far away. Tal cautiously crossed the grass to it, and studied it before he stepped onto it. It was made of bricks, but not normal ones. These were violet crystal and had Sunstone fragments suspended in them. As his foot came down, the bricks under it sparkled, but nothing sinister happened.

Adras hovered in the air behind Tal.

"Something smells funny," whispered the Storm Shepherd. "Oily."

Tal sniffed the air, but he couldn't smell anything oily. All he could smell was the fresh scent of grass and the pleasant perfume of the flowers that grew on the tall bushes ahead.

Tal walked along the path for a while. It looked like it circumnavigated the island. Other paths ran off it, into the interior. One of them headed in the direction of the house.

Tal took it. He walked a little slower as the path headed between two overhanging flower bushes. Something about the whole place made him uneasy. Perhaps it was the moonlight, he thought. It made everything look creepy.

He took a few more steps before he realized what it was.

There was a light breeze blowing from behind his back.

But the bushes were leaning toward him.

Tal stopped and looked at them. They were taller than he was. Big bushes with broad clusters of green leaves. Both had two large red flowers about two-thirds of the way up.

"They're only plants," Tal said aloud. "Only plants."

But he didn't walk toward them. As he watched, first one flower then another slowly swiveled to face him. Then, with a horrible sucking sound, both bushes lifted their roots out of the ground and glided forward, rustling. The roots they moved on were sharp and pointed, more like multiple talons than anything else.

Tal backed away. But he had only gone a few paces when Adras said, "Uh-oh."

Tal looked behind. Two of the statues he'd seen from the air were coming down the path. They were humanoid, a little larger than an adult Chosen, and made of the same golden metal as the Ruin Ship. As they closed in, Tal noticed the oily smell Adras had mentioned before. They moved like Tal and Adras in the Chromatic armor. Slowly and clumsily.

"Time to fly," said Tal, reaching up his arms. Adras swooped down and grabbed him, and this time it really hurt — because Tal's feet wouldn't leave the path.

He looked down and saw strands of violet wrapping themselves around his ankles, forming shackles of light.

The flower creatures glided forward, piercing roots questing ahead of them. The statues shuddered up behind, their massive fists rising and falling.

"Let go, I'm stuck! Try to hold them off!"

Adras let go. Instantly Tal focused on his Sunstone. If he could make a Violet Key he could unlock the shackles on his ankles. Thanks to Lokar, he had some idea of what he had to do.

But could he do it before the statues clubbed him down or the flower creatures stabbed him?

·CHAPTER·
SIXTEEN

Malen kept working on Crow for several hours after the Freefolk left to gather airweed and take it to the Icecarl advance guard. Milla watched the Crone's quick and clever hands for a while, then decided to make sure Jarnil hadn't tried to sneak away.

She found him asleep in his bed. Milla looked down at him, wondering again whether she should do anything. She was about to leave when something triggered a memory. Jarnil was sleeping in an odd posture. He had his hands linked on his chest, under the blanket.

Milla pulled the blanket back. As she'd suspected, his hands were clasped around a Sunstone.

Jarnil wasn't asleep. He'd gone to Aenir. Without leaving a Spiritshadow to guard the body he left behind, because he didn't have one anymore. It had been taken from him in the Hall of Nightmares.

Yet even though he had been cast out and made an Underfolk, and eventually one of the Freefolk, in the end it hadn't been enough to break his lifelong loyalty. There was only one reason Jarnil would have gone to Aenir.

He was going to warn the Chosen about the Icecarl invasion.

Milla's knife came out of her sleeve and into her hand. She held it lightly, poised above Jarnil's throat. Then she sighed and put it away. Nothing would be gained by killing Jarnil's body. She didn't know if it would kill him in Aenir, and in any case, he was a brave man to do what he had done. Plus, he was asleep and defenseless. There would only be dishonor if she slew him now.

Milla climbed back up to the central courtyard and splashed some water from the well on her face. When Jarnil gave them a warning, the Chosen would swiftly return. They would also learn about this fortress. If Milla stayed here, she could be cut off from her forces, the Freefolk fortress being too easily besieged with its single bridge over the lava crevasse.

But her knowledge of the Castle and the Under-

117

folk levels in particular was too limited. How could she be a War-Chief if she didn't know the territory where her people would fight?

"I need maps," she shouted angrily, releasing the tension she felt at her own mistake in leaving Jarnil unwatched. "Where can I find maps?"

A splash from the well answered her question. Instantly, Milla leaped back from the rim, her Merwin-horn sword and dagger in her hands.

A door-sized rectangle of crystal slowly floated up through the water. It was horizontal at first, but then it levitated upright, water splashing down on every side. Even after the water fell, its face was liquid and shining.

Icecarl runes formed upon its surface.

"Maps may be found in many places within the Castle. I have many maps within me."

For once Milla stared. This was the Codex of the Chosen, the magical artifact she and Tal had risked their lives to bring back from Aenir. They had left it hidden in the Mausoleum higher in the Castle, only to learn from Ebbitt that the Codex could wander of its own accord.

"You have come back," Milla said.

The Codex didn't answer. It was its nature to only answer questions.

"How do I get to the Underfolk levels from here?" Milla asked.

Silver lines appeared on the shining surface of the Codex. They drew a map. Milla studied it intently. There was another way out of the Fortress of the Freefolk, she saw, but it was narrow and difficult and led only to a distant part of the heatways.

"Where is the best place for a raiding party of five hundred Icecarls to gather in the Underfolk levels so they can quickly attack the higher Chosen levels?"

Another map formed, showing a huge chamber labeled as The Assembly of the Miners. Milla smiled as she studied the map. Even if the Chosen did come back, the Codex would help her defeat them. There were so many secret ways and passages that the Chosen wouldn't know. The Codex, on the other hand, knew everything.

If she could make sure it stayed around.

"Malen!" she called, half turning away. "Malen!"

As she turned back, the Codex sank into the well again. Milla snatched at it, and for a moment held a corner fast. But it shrank under her fingers and slipped away. In seconds the Codex was the size of a large fish and it zipped away like one, down into the deep waters of the well.

Malen came out as Milla scooped vainly at the well, spraying the Crone with water.

"War-Chief!" exclaimed Malen, affronted.

"The Codex! It was here!"

Malen rushed to the well, but there was nothing to be seen. She looked at Milla, her blue eyes already clouding over as she prepared to share whatever Milla said with the other Crones.

"The Codex of the Chosen," said Milla. "It was here. It came out of the well. I asked it to show me maps of the Castle. Tell the Crones with the advance guard to tell the Shield Maidens to ask the Freefolk to show them the way to the Assembly of the Miners on Underfolk Level Seven. We will meet there. Also . . . I have made a mistake. Jarnil has gone to Aenir to warn the Chosen."

Milla paused and waited for Malen to speak. But the young Crone was silent for some time. When she did talk, it was with the strange, gestalt voice of all the Crones, the voice that sent shivers down Milla's spine.

"You must keep the Codex if it comes again. It is of the highest importance."

Malen stopped talking and nearly fell into the well. Milla steadied her.

"Sorry," said Malen. She suddenly sounded like

her nose was blocked. "I'm not . . . not used to carrying the Voice. I've only had the basic lessons."

For once Malen didn't sound like a Crone. She sounded like a young Icecarl with a touch of the chill-fever, an Icecarl who wasn't too confident she could do what had to be done, but would try anyway.

Milla liked her the better for it.

"How is Crow?" she asked.

"I think he will recover," answered Malen. She coughed and stood straighter. The blue in her eyes grew brighter and she sounded more confident. "He will sleep normally now, and should be able to speak when he wakes."

"Can he be moved?" asked Milla. "If Bennem carries him?"

Malen frowned. "If he must."

"And Ebbitt, can he be moved?"

"Who knows? He is old and has overexerted himself. If he were an Icecarl, I think he would give himself to the Ice."

"But he is not," said Milla. "And the Castle is not so hard a place for the old as a ship. He is also very wise and powerful with the Chosen's light magic."

"It is different here," Malen acknowledged. She shivered and said, "I fear that it will change us, coming here."

Milla was silent. She had been changed beyond recognition already, so much she hardly knew who she was anymore. So few things were certain. One was her responsibility as War-Chief of the Icecarls.

"We will move," she ordered. "All of us, before the Chosen return. Bennem will carry Crow, Odris will carry Jarnil, and Ebbitt will ride on his Spirit-shadow's back. We will go to the Hall of Miners to meet the advance guard — and prepare for the attack."

·CHAPTER· SEVENTEEN

Adras swooped down and tried to topple the closest statue. It rocked back momentarily, but even the Storm Shepherd's strength could not prevent it from moving forward. Its mighty fists slammed into Adras's cloudy chest and sank in.

"Owwgh!" gasped Adras. He reeled back. "That hurt!"

The flower-creatures were advancing, too. Long, sharp roots slid ahead of them, as the trunks and branches crept inexorably forward.

Tal didn't look. He kept concentrating on his Sunstone and the shackles of light. They were violet, and all he had to do was find the right Violet Key to make them let him go. He had to bring the correct light forth from his Sunstone.

"I can't . . . can't stop them!" puffed Adras as he was flung aside by a huge golden arm.

Tal heard the Storm Shepherd's voice as if it were far away. All his concentration, every scrap of willpower was focused on his Sunstone. Light shone there, first red, then it flickered through orange, yellow, green, blue, indigo . . . and violet.

But it was a weak violet, lacking the fire and strength of the true color. Tal bent all his thought upon it, trying to intensify the light, to make it true. He had to have pure violet to make his key and escape.

The statues grew closer. A sharp root, ahead of the rest, sliced across Tal's shin, drawing blood. He ignored it. The light was intensifying. It was almost there. Another root slashed across his leg. A flower bent toward him and some part of Tal's mind noted that its petals were as sharp as steel as they came toward his face.

Then something clicked inside Tal's head. He felt totally attuned with his Sunstone, as if he and it were the only things that existed in the whole world.

Violet, thought Tal.

The Sunstone flared into bright, pure violet light.

It grew brighter and brighter — Tal had to close his eyes and shield his face with his arm. Violet light was everywhere, all around, and he couldn't see, couldn't make it undo his shackles. Any second the flower would cut his face and the statues would smash him to the ground . . .

The light faded. No flower cut came, no crushing blow. Tal opened his eyes and let his arm fall. The flower-creatures were retreating to their groves along the path. The statues had turned around and were lumbering back to resume their stolid poses. Adras was floating just off the path, rubbing his chest and groaning.

There was still a faint remnant of violet light. Tal looked down. His legs were only lightly scratched and the blood was already drying. The light shackles around his ankles were gone, and the path sparkled innocently. The violet light came from his Sunstone.

Tal held his hand close to his face. The Sunstone had changed. It had been generally yellow with flecks of red before, and occasional twinkles of all the other colors. Now it was a pure deep violet, all the way through, down into hidden depths it hadn't had before.

"Thanks," said Adras. "Those statues *hurt*."

"I . . . I don't know what I did," said Tal. He let his hand fall. The Sunstone dimmed a little, but his fingers were still washed in violet light. "Come on."

There were a lot more flower-creatures along the path, and several more statues. Tal felt a strong urge to run past them, but he didn't. He just kept walking. The flower-creatures rustled as he passed, but made no move to attack. The statues' heads swiveled to watch him, but didn't step off their plinths.

It made for a very creepy progress in the moonlight. Tal kept expecting a flower-creature to go from a rustle to a sudden stab, and the statues to suddenly move and bar his way.

Finally, they came to the house. As Tal had seen from the air, only the courtyard was lit up. The crystal leaves that were woven into the canopy above the courtyard shone green and silver in the moonlight, and tinkled in the light breeze.

There were several people in the courtyard, despite the fact that it was very late. Or very early, depending on how you thought about it.

Tal paused next to a flower-creature to get a proper look before he went into the open. It wasn't a very successful reconnaissance as he kept one eye on the closest branches and tried to do his spying with the other.

Because the crystal leaves hung over the sides as well as making up a canopy, it was hard to see what was going on. As far as Tal could tell, there were two people sitting down in the very center of the courtyard, and two others waiting on them, occasionally going back and forth to the house.

The two sitting down were probably Chosen, as Tal caught brief flashes of light from their Sunstones, brighter and differently colored than the ones that were set in the corner-posts. The two servants . . . he wasn't sure about. They didn't seem to be human-shaped.

One of the sitting Chosen had to be the Empress, Tal thought. With a courtier, and two servants of some kind. Who else could it be?

He looked nervously around for the guards. But there didn't seem to be anyone else nearby. The house was dark and quiet. Perhaps here the Empress relied totally on the flower-creatures, the statues, and the magic in the paths.

So there was no one to stop him from walking over, bowing before the Empress, and giving light. He could tell her about Sushin, the Veil, his father . . . everything.

"I need a drink," whispered Adras. Or in his idea of a whisper. It made Tal jump into the flower-creature. If it hadn't leaned away he would have been sliced to pieces.

"I don't understand this place," Tal whispered

back when he recovered his balance. In some ways it was worse than being out on the Ice. At least there he knew he didn't know anything. Here in the Chosen Enclave, he felt like he ought to be more knowledgeable. He should know why the Sunstone harpoons were in the lakebed, he should know why his Sunstone had gone Violet, he should know why the guards of the Empress's island had suffered a change of heart.

But he didn't. And at this very last minute, he was having doubts about the wisdom of going before the Empress. Yes, she did have the power to put everything right. But he hadn't followed the correct procedures to see her, even if it was impossible to do so with Sushin in control of the Guards and so much else. It wasn't the Chosen way to just saunter across in the middle of the night and address the very highest of the Chosen.

Yet there was no other way. This was the choice he had made. He had to be brave and take the opportunity.

He stood up and walked across the grass. Adras billowed along behind him. They went to an arched gateway and stepped under the canopy of crystal leaves.

Tal looked across the courtyard. Two slim, long-armed semi-human creatures with large green eyes and fuzzy black fur looked back at him. One carried a silver tray with a bottle on it, the other a golden tray with two crystal goblets. Neither creature seemed at all perturbed by Tal and Adras. After a moment's glance, they looked away again.

There were also two Chosen, seated in the middle of the canopy. They paid the new arrivals no attention at all. They were both engrossed in a game of Beastmaker. The game was in its final stages, all cards played and the beasts already created in the battlecircle. A star-shaped thing with many mouths was wrapped around a scaly, two-headed insectoid. The latter had a long tail-sting that it struck with every few seconds, hitting itself as often as its opponent.

Both the Chosen players wore flowing violet robes and many Sunstones. They were both indescribably ancient, extremely thin, and had very long white hair. It took Tal a moment to work out that the one with the violet cap trimmed with Sunstones was female, and thus almost certainly the Empress, and that her bareheaded counterpart was male. They were obviously closely related. Brother and sister, or perhaps mother and son. They were so old it was hard to pick any difference in their ages.

Tal approached, but they paid him no attention. When he was only a few stretches away, he sank to one knee, raised his Sunstone, and gave them respectful light.

At the same time, the insectoid beast expired. The star creature flexed up on one point and did a strange little dance. Then the game was over, and both creatures vanished in a stream of tiny sparks of light that circled round and round the polished gameboard and back into the deck of cards.

Only then did the two Chosen turn to face Tal. Each held out a hand, the Empress her right and her relative his left. The two semi-human servants placed a goblet in each hand and then poured out something frothy and black.

They drank and threw the goblets behind them, which were dexterously caught by the servants.

Tal waited, still on one knee. Eventually, he gave light again. He'd meant to give an orange glow appropriate to his station, but somehow it came out violet.

This got the Empress's attention.

"Oh! It's him!" she wailed. "It's him!"

·CHAPTER·
EIGHTEEN

"No it isn't, Ildi," said the other Chosen. "Don't be stupid. Who are you, boy? You look familiar. Gronnius's son?"

"I am Tal Graile-Rerem," announced Tal. "I bear important news for Her Imperial Highness."

"Never heard of you," said the man. "What are you doing here with important news? Tell it to Sushin. We're busy. Got a Beastmaker series to finish. Best of a hundred."

"Yes, go away," pronounced the Empress. At least Tal was pretty certain she was the Empress. He'd only ever seen her in the distance before, at important events, when she wore full robes of state. But he thought Ebbitt had said her name was Kathilde, and the man had just called her Ildi.

"Um, you *are* Her Imperial Highness?" he asked hesitantly.

"Of course I am . . . that is, we are," the old woman retorted. "Why does this doubt . . . this treachery . . . this carping disbelief continue?"

"I don't doubt, Highness," Tal assured her hastily. "It's only I've never been so close to you before, and your . . . um . . . radiance is blinding."

"Well, that is true," the Empress conceded. "You are a well-brought-up boy. But I cannot recall your parents' names among our Violet personages. Perhaps they are newly risen? We are so busy that we fear we get a trifle behind from time to time."

Tal glanced down at the Sunstone on his finger, and its glowing violet pulse. Obviously the Empress thought he was of the Violet order, the child of a Shadowlord and lady. Time to change the subject.

"Highness, I bring grave news," he said again. "There is a plot against the Chosen by the shadows of Aenir. Some of the Keystones have been unsealed, and the Veil is threatened. Our whole world is in danger."

The Empress smiled and shook her finger at Tal.

"Now, now, if you want to present a light-puppet drama to us, you must apply to our Light Vizier first."

"And I'll tell you straight off that your story sounds stupid, it's been done before, and anyway we'd rather play Beastmaker than watch some incompetent stripling fumbling about with light puppets," said the man.

"You're the Light Vizier?" asked Tal. He had a terrible sinking feeling in his chest. They were both so old, and they didn't appear to be listening to him at all!

"Uthern Lalis-Offin, Light Vizier to . . . to her," replied the man. He waved his hand vaguely and a faint violet glow came off his Sunstone.

He leaned forward and almost fell out of his chair, both furry servants arriving only just in time to catch him.

"Confidentially, my boy," he whispered, "I'm the elder brother. I should have been Emperor after we kicked Mercur out. But *she* was in more with the Violet and the Indigo."

Tal's nose wrinkled as Uthern leaned back. The Light Vizier wasn't just old. He was drunk, and so, by the look of her, was the Empress.

"I'm not pretending," he said urgently. "I'm telling the truth. Sushin is in league with the Aenirans and they are unsealing the Keystones!"

At Sushin's name, Empress and Light Vizier

looked at each other like children caught in a Lector's glare.

"Not our business," announced the Empress. "Ceremonial duties only. Made quite clear. Long ago. You may leave us."

"But you have to listen," urged Tal. He jumped to his feet and stood over the Empress. "You have to do something! My father is trapped inside the Orange Keystone! Lokar is trapped inside the Red. Look!"

He undid the knot in his shirt and pulled out the Red Keystone. It flared brightly as he raised it, and both the Empress and Uthern whimpered and tried to shield their eyes.

"We don't want it!" shrieked the Empress.

Tal stared down at the two of them, cowering in their chairs. He couldn't believe these were the highest and mightiest of the Chosen, the pinnacle of Castle society. What was wrong with them?

"Look into the stone," he pleaded. "Your Highness, you have to use the Violet Keystone to release Lokar! You have to."

"Haven't got it," whimpered the Empress. "Foundation of doubt."

Tal lowered the Red Keystone and stepped back.

"What do you mean you haven't got it?" he whispered. "I've come so far . . . gone through so much . . ."

"She never had it," said Uthern with a vindictive look at his sister. "Mercur had a back way out, all the way down to the Underfolk levels. He took it. The Violet Keystone, the Claw of Ramellan, the secret knowledge. But I struck him as he ran."

The old man raised a skinny arm and mimed throwing a bolt of light.

"I never had it," repeated the Empress. "No one could know. We agreed, Uthern. But you told the shadow."

"I didn't," hissed Uthern. "It was you, you."

"What shadow?" asked Tal slowly. "What did you tell the shadow?"

135

"Sharrakor, Sharrakor, Sharrakor," crooned the Empress. "How we wish he had never slithered across our path."

"Sharrakor?" asked Tal. "Your Spiritshadow?"

The Empress and Uthern laughed, a mad giggle that raised the hair on the back of Tal's head.

"Not mine, no, no," cackled the Empress. She gestured at the furred servants behind her. "There are our Spiritshadows. No one to guard us in the Castle. No loyal Spiritshadows to make sure we survive. Sharrakor is his own master."

Tal stared aghast at the little black humanoids. Apart from the fact that as bound servants they should be guarding the two Chosen's bodies back in the Castle, they were obviously completely harmless and were totally unsuitable to be Spiritshadows to any Violet Chosen, let alone the Empress and the Light Vizier.

Yet everyone thought Sharrakor was the bound and true servant of the Empress. Sharrakor, who was regarded as the most powerful Spiritshadow of them all.

"And Sushin?" he asked. "What is Sushin?"

"Shadow-pawn," said Uthern. He had stopped laughing and was weeping now, the tears sliding down his aged and wrinkled cheeks. "Shadow-pawn of Sharrakor."

"You have betrayed us," said Tal. He couldn't believe it. They'd undermined everything. It was their fault that his father was trapped in the Orange Keystone. They were ultimately responsible for the disappearances and the deaths. The Pit and the perversion of the Hall of Nightmares. "You have betrayed us all to the shadows."

"No," said Kathild. "I am the Empress of the Chosen. I am Most High!"

"No," said Uthern, but his voice quavered and

the tears still fell. "I am Light Vizier. Nothing will change. The Chosen will go on. The Castle will stand. The Veil will hold."

"No they won't!" screamed Tal. He was almost sobbing himself, but with rage, not sorrow. "I should kill you both! It's what the Icecarls would do to traitors!"

He stepped back still farther and raised his own Sunstone. It swirled with violet light. Tal fed his anger into it, and the violet light grew and strengthened. Tal didn't know what he was going to do, or what spell he could cast. He just let all his rage, frustration, and fear fly into the stone.

Violet lightning began to spit out of the Sunstone, crackling and flashing. It shot out and around Tal, spinning a barrier of violet streaks. Tal tried to make it stop circling and strike the two Chosen, but it wouldn't be directed. It rose higher and higher until there was a spinning storm of violet lightning bolts flashing over Tal's head.

The Empress and the Light Vizier stared up at it, white-faced. Then they fell out of their chairs and prostrated themselves at Tal's feet, sobbing and clutching at his ankles.

"Spare us! Spare us, Mercur, Ramellan, whoever you are!"

·CHAPTER·
NINETEEN

Tal stared down at the two Chosen, then up at the crackling violet light above his head. It had formed into the shape he knew well. The Jagged Lightning Crown, worn by the Empress on the Day of Ascension and Dark Return.

Why was this strange light replica of the crown hovering over *his* head?

"I'm so sorry, Highness," sobbed Uthern. "She made me do it!"

The Empress hissed and scratched at Uthern. In a second, they were rolling around on the ground, weakly kicking and hitting each other, more like children or baby animals than people.

Tal bent down and pulled them apart. They were so thin and light, he could have picked one up in each hand. He sat them back in their chairs and their servants hurried forward to straighten their clothes and hair.

"Why do you call me Highness?" he asked. The anger had all gone out of him now, though the crown of violet light remained. He felt cold and hard now, without anger.

Or mercy.

"You wield the Violet Keystone," whispered brother and sister together. "Are you Ramellan come again, to punish us?"

Tal looked at the stone on his finger, now revealed in all its Violet glory. He remembered the skeleton in the heatway tunnel. It must have been the late Emperor Mercur, who had not quite managed to escape the traitors who had supplanted him.

He also remembered Ebbitt splitting the Sunstone. What he wore on his finger now was only half the Violet Keystone. The other half was probably atop the mast of the Far-Raiders ship. Or lost with Milla upon the Ice, he thought with a pang.

But even half the Violet Keystone might be enough to release Lokar and his father. It might be enough to reseal the Keystones and save the Veil. It might be enough to rally the Chosen and turn them against Sushin and Sharrakor.

But only if Tal had the courage and the strength

to use the Keystone properly. Now there really was no one else he could go to. It was all up to him. He had to make the right decisions, starting right now.

Tal felt like he had before he decided to climb the Red Tower, in a life that seemed long ago. That simple decision had changed everything. Now he stood on the brink once more, in the frozen moment before he did something that could not be undone.

He felt every muscle in his body tense, as if he were a spring being compressed as far as it would go. What would happen when it was released?

Tal stared at the two cringing Chosen. What was he to do with them? What was his next step? He couldn't kill them, he realized. He might not really be a Chosen anymore, but he wasn't an Icecarl, either.

He was prevented from making a decision by a shout from Adras, who had drifted off to suck up water from an ornamental pool nearby.

Tal turned to see what was the matter. As he did so, Kathilde and Uthern both leaped forward, drawing crystal daggers from the arms of their chairs.

"Die!" they screamed.

Tal twisted back, but he was too slow to do anything else. The daggers flashed down — and were met by bolts of violet lightning from the crown above his head. Crystal exploded into powder, and then more lightning struck, straight at the hearts of the Empress and the Light Vizier!

Tal reeled back and was caught by Adras as the violet lightning jumped the gap between Kathilde and Uthern and struck their servants as well. There was a tremendous flash, a boom louder than any of Adras's thunder, and all the crystal leaves were blown off the canopy.

Tal and Adras were thrown to the ground. Through slitted eyes Tal saw Kathilde and Uthern struck again and again by bolts of violet lightning. It played over their bodies, striking every part of them, the flashes blinding and the thunderclaps deafening. Sunstones on the Chosen's clothing absorbed some of the lightning, and for a few seconds the two continued to struggle, to try to get away. But in the end the last Sunstone exploded into dust and the Empress Kathilde and her Light Vizier were still.

The violet crown that had been above Tal's head drifted across to them, and the bands of light rearranged themselves into a vaguely human shape. It hovered above the dead Chosen, raised its arms in triumph, and disappeared in a fall of violet sparks.

"Did you do that?" asked Adras. "I liked the lightning."

"No," said Tal wearily. "That, I think, was the death curse of the Emperor Mercur. I just delivered it."

He got up and dusted himself off. He didn't go and look at the bodies. There wasn't much left of them, and the ground around them was still smoking.

"What were you going on about just then?" asked Tal.

"Hmmm?" asked Adras. He was inspecting the burn marks on a nearby pole. "Oh, a ship."

He pointed. Tal looked. Sure enough, a large boat was approaching the island. It was brightly lit with Sunstones and crammed with the Empress's Guards and other Chosen. A familiar rotund figure was standing at the bow.

"Sushin," groaned Tal. Now was not the time to confront him, or to try to win the Chosen over. Not with the Empress and the Light Vizier dead at his feet.

"I hope you haven't had so much water you can't fly," Tal said.

"Why?"

"Because we have to fly, of course!" shouted Tal.

"There's no need to shout," sniffed Adras. "Where are we going?"

Tal shook his head. He felt incredibly tired again.

"I don't know. Away from here before that boat lands."

"Too late for that," said Adras. "It just did."

"It can't have," said Tal. He didn't bother to look. "It was hundreds of stretches away."

"No," explained Adras patiently. "The other ship. The one I didn't see before."

Tal looked. Another boat full of Guards had grounded on the western shore. The first Chosen were jumping off the bow. They saw him, and an angry shout went up.

Tal's tiredness disappeared. He turned to run, tugging at Adras's hand.

"Come on," he shouted, holding up both arms. "Running takeoff!"

"I feel sick," announced Adras. But he pushed off the ground and grabbed Tal's arms as he lifted him into the sky. The very low part of the sky. Tal was dragged along the ground, and only saved from being sliced apart because two flower-creatures leaned over backward to let him past.

"Higher!" Tal screamed. For a moment his feet rested on the shoulders of a golden statue. He jumped off and they gained a bit of height, only to lose it again as Adras groaned and dipped.

They were almost at the lake on the far side of the island when Adras finally managed to get properly airborne. He kept heading toward the crater rim, mindful of all the Chosen and their Sunstones that were behind him.

Tal breathed a sigh of relief, only to lose it in panic as he realized something truly horrible.

He'd dropped the Red Keystone when they were knocked over back in the courtyard.

·CHAPTER·
TWENTY

"Take us high," said Tal bitterly. "Then you can drop me."

"How high?" asked Adras.

"High enough," muttered Tal. How could he have been so stupid? He'd been so careful not to lose the Red Keystone. That Icecarl Crone had prophesied truly when she said, "Sunstones fall from you, yet into other's hands."

"Um, Tal, why am I going to drop you?" asked Adras.

"You're not," said Tal shortly. "I'm just angry at myself. I don't really mean for you to drop me. Is that cloud up there? Let's join that for a while."

"Sure," said Adras. There was a long strand of cloud drifting over the crater. "Why are you angry at yourself?"

Tal bit back an angry response. There was no point in yelling at Adras.

"I dropped the Red Keystone," he said dully. "I've practically killed Lokar, just like everyone else."

"The Red Keystone?" asked Adras. "Is that the red Sunstone?"

Tal took a deep, slow breath. "Yes, it is the red Sunstone."

"Oh, I picked that up," said Adras. "I thought you'd want it."

"You picked it up?" Tal repeated. He looked up at the Storm Shepherd, who was smiling down at him. "Where is it?"

"I put it in my pocket."

"Your pocket? You haven't got a pocket... um... have you?"

"When I want to have a pocket I have a pocket," replied Adras proudly. "Look!"

He let go of one of Tal's arms and the Chosen boy swung wildly underneath. But Tal didn't panic. He just gripped a little tighter himself.

Adras reached into his stomach area and two big puffy fingers pulled out a small red-glowing Sunstone. He started to hand it over to Tal.

"No, you keep it for now," said Tal urgently. "You've earned the right to look after it."

He didn't add that the last thing he wanted to do while hanging beneath a Storm Shepherd a thousand stretches up was take an irreplaceable Sunstone from two oversized cloud fingers and try to tie it in his shirt.

When they rendezvoused with the cloud, Tal had Adras stay a fraction beneath it, so he could watch what was going on down below. There was a lot of activity, not only on the Empress's island, but all over the Chosen Enclave. Sunstones were flaring brightly everywhere, in houses and on walkways and bridges. It was a colorful sight from a safe distance.

While the death of the Empress was bound to cause a stir, Tal couldn't figure out why absolutely everybody was dashing around. There were even Chosen running back from the tunnel that went through the crater wall.

Tal and Adras stayed with the cloud for some time. The sun had risen and the last of the night darkness was slipping from the crater below when Tal finally figured out what was going on.

"They're going back," he said, disbelief in his voice. "The Chosen are going back to the Castle. But it's months yet to Dark Return!"

Even the death of the Empress would not prompt a return to the Castle. It was unheard of. From the Day of Ascension to the Day of Dark Return, all

Chosen were in Aenir. It was as simple as that. But there was no mistaking what was going on below. The Orders were gathering in their respective areas. Tal could see the different colors in their Sunstones as they assembled along the major bridges. There was his Orange Order on the West Bridge, every single one of them.

Tal peered down. He wished he had a telescope. There were a number of litters with the Orange Order, for the sick and the infirm. His mother would be lying on one. She had to be. He refused to consider that she might now be dead.

A bunch of Chosen around the edge of the Orange ranks suddenly disappeared, leaving a prismatic afterimage. Tal blinked. That was even more unusual than the fact that the Chosen were returning. There was a set order to going back to the Castle. Red went first, from lowest to highest, and then it went in order of seniority through the other colors.

A group of Blue Chosen suddenly shone and then they were gone, too. Then a couple of Indigo, and a bunch of Yellows.

"Let's go lower," Tal instructed. "I need to see this."

They sank lower, but no one looked up. They were all too intent on getting back to the Castle.

Tal watched as the transfers became even more

confused. People seemed to be transferring back as soon as they were ready. A lot of children and sick Chosen were being sent back even when they weren't ready. Tal saw one little boy running away from his mother when he was struck by a kaleido-scopic whorl that signaled the transfer.

It took Tal a few minutes to realize that what he was seeing was a panic. The Chosen were desperate to return to the Castle and the Dark World. But why? Had the Spiritshadows already revolted? Surely that would be accompanied by an attack here in Aenir as well?

Whatever was going on, Tal knew it was an op-portunity for him. He looked down at the steadily thinning ranks of the Chosen. If it was chaos here, with everyone translating back, it would be even worse in the Castle.

Now was the time to go back and give the water spider antidote to his mother . . . if he hadn't lost it. Tal felt the other knot in his shirt, the one he had never undone. Two vials of precious antidote were there. Provided they weren't harmed by the trans-fer to Aenir and then back, they should bring Graile out of her coma and make her well.

"Take us to the crater wall," said Tal. "We're go-ing back home."

"This is home," said Adras.

"The Dark World," said Tal. "You'll be a Spirit-shadow again."

"Hhmmph," snorted Adras. But he headed for the crater wall.

Home, thought Tal. Where was home now? Almost everything he had thought was true about the Chosen and the Castle was a lie. The Empress had proved to be a usurper and a coward, her Light Vizier likewise. The Dark Vizier was the puppet of a shadow.

And back in the Castle, like a dark stain across his life, there was the memory of his failures, the accident he had caused, and the deaths for which he was responsible.

Atonement was the answer, Tal thought bleakly. He had to make up for what he had done. He must release Lokar and his father and the other Guardians trapped in the Keystones. He must defeat Sushin and Sharrakor and save the Veil. Not just for his people, but also for the Icecarls. He owed Milla that, and more.

It was all up to him.

"Fly to that ledge," he said, pointing. "We will transfer back from there."

·CHAPTER·
TWENTY–ONE

The Assembly of the Miners was a vast natural cave that had long ago been adapted into a splendid auditorium. Its sloping floor had been shaped into broad terraces and the protruding rock at its southern end sculpted into an imposing pulpit.

In its heyday, during the construction of the Castle, it had regularly held gatherings of twenty or thirty thousand people. That time was long gone, and much of the vast chamber was dim now, the Sunstones on the ceiling far above faded.

The Underfolk used a fraction of one of the terraces to store stone bottles of oil, but otherwise the hall was deserted.

The Assembly was an ideal gathering place for Milla and her Icecarls. It had many entrances and exits, most importantly a very broad corridor leading to the Clear Ascendor, one of the major stairways of the Castle, that led all the way from the lowest Underfolk levels to the beginning of the Violet.

Milla's strange cavalcade of Crone, Spiritshadows, damaged Bennem, spirit-departed Jarnil, dozing Ebbitt, and wounded Crow had arrived in the Assembly without difficulty. They had seen Underfolk on the way, but they had quickly scuttled away when they saw the Spiritshadows.

Apart from them, the lower levels of the Castle were quiet. They saw no other Spiritshadows, and there was no sign of any general alarm. There had not been any attempts to close the many doors and gates that had probably not moved for centuries, or decades at least.

Malen made her patients as comfortable as she could near the pulpit, while Milla and Adras traversed the terraces of the Assembly. Satisfied that there was no ambush there, and that it would be easy to both attack or retreat from, Milla returned to the others to wait for her first warriors to arrive, and to speak to the Crones through Malen.

It wasn't a really long wait — less than eight Chosen hours — but it felt like one. Milla was acutely aware that the Chosen, forewarned by Jarnil, could return at any time. Or the free Spiritshadows already in the Castle might decide to attack both the Chosen and her little band. Milla wondered what the bound Spiritshadows would do if they were confronted by their brethren. Would their bindings force them to fight? After all, the Chosen employed a variation of the Prayer of Asteyr, which, as far as Milla knew, could not be thwarted.

The free Spiritshadows probably wouldn't attack until the Veil was destroyed. They would have to bring a vast host from Aenir to overcome both the Chosen and their bound Spiritshadows. They couldn't do that until the Veil was destroyed and the light made them more powerful.

The question was, how damaged was the Veil already? Milla wished Crow was conscious, so she could ask him what he had learned in the Red Tower. She knew that he and Tal had gotten the Keystone, but not much else.

A slight sound alerted Milla to movement near one of the nearer entrances. She crouched, knife and Talon ready. Odris slid across the ground to her right side and reared up.

An Icecarl slipped around the corner. A Shield Maiden. She saw Milla and gave her the good-hunting sign, two fingers held straight down and whisked to the side. Milla returned the sign.

The Shield Maiden disappeared back beyond the doorway. A moment later, she returned. A Shield Mother came next, followed by a tide of Shield Maidens and hunters. The Shield Mother clapped her fists briefly at Milla, then turned to direct her followers to fan out as they entered the chamber, tapping each one as they passed and pointing them in different directions.

All the Icecarls carried airweed draped across their hunting packs, in case they had to fight their way back through the heatways. Milla was pleased to see that forethought.

More and more Icecarls poured in. Another four Shield Mothers arrived, each clapping their fists to Milla before joining the first Shield Mother to confer briefly, then direct their Maidens or Hunters to join different groups.

Milla waited patiently. This was always the way of the hunt. Only when everyone was in a proper position would the lesser leaders come to the Icecarl who led them all.

She was surprised by the next arrival. A gigantic Icecarl, his chest and arms bare, bent his head to fit through the door. His feet and all his skin save a small circle around his nose, mouth, and eyes were stained a deep, rich blue. He wore only trousers, his feet bare. The trousers were made of the shimmery, scaled skin of a rare and extremely dangerous Norr-worm. Around his waist was a heavy chain of golden metal, the links as thick as Milla's hands.

Only one Icecarl went barefoot on the Ice and lived to walk again. He had to be the famous Sword-Thane Jarek Bloodswimmer. Not only had he killed two Norrworms, he'd had to swim in their blood for three sleeps, until it seeped out of the ice cave where they died. The blood had permanently transformed his skin, making it very tough and resistant to cold and fire.

Jarek was a Wilder. The chain was his weapon.

At his side was a small woman, who at first glance looked like a regular Shield Maiden, until Milla noticed she wore her furs in a strange fashion, had six differently shaped knives at her belt, and her low boots were also made of Norrworm hide.

Milla knew her, too, for her legend was twined in Jarek's own. She was Kirr, a Shield Maiden who had been given leave to wander with the Sword-Thane. She was Jarek's companion, the only Icecarl who could control, at least a little, his Wilder rages. He never harmed her, and she could bring him out of the fury. The Crones considered this to be an important service, so she was not required to join a Hand.

Jarek and Kirr saw Milla, and clapped their fists to her before heading up to watch yet another entrance. Milla was surprised, caught staring at them. She was almost too slow to clap her fists in return. She had seen some other, less famous Sword-Thanes on the Mountain, but had no idea that Jarek and Kirr had joined them.

More Shield Maidens came in, then two Freefolk, Gill and Ferek. They started to head toward Milla, then hesitated, not sure they should approach, because the Shield Mothers hadn't done so.

Milla beckoned them over.

"Don't worry," she said. "The Shield Mothers are just getting everyone sorted out. Where are Clovil and Inkie?"

"They're showing some of your people the air-weed lake," Gill reported. She kept staring at all the arriving Icecarls, obviously excited by the activity. "Then they're going to try and convince some of the Fatalists that the time has finally come to break free!"

"Good," said Milla. "I'm glad you have come back, because I wanted to ask you if you will be guides. We will need you, and as many other Freefolk as you can gather, to show us the way to different parts of the Castle. Particularly the Chosen levels."

"Sure!" exclaimed Gill. "My parents were table-washers for the Red, Orange, and Yellow Commons. I know those levels really well."

Ferek was silent. Milla saw him swallow and twitch nervously.

"Though we will need someone here, too," she added quickly. "This will be our ship-home, for the Crones and the wounded. We will need a Freefolk here, one who knows these lower levels. It's an important job. Perhaps, Ferek, you will stay here and do that?"

Milla had once valued courage above all else. But since then she had been in the Hall of Nightmares, and she knew what that place could do to a child, one who did not know how to call the Crones to save them from bad dreams. Ferek was such a child.

"Yes, yes, I will," said Ferek, looking relieved.

"Good," Milla replied. She saw the Shield Mothers turn and approach. There were twenty of them now, which meant twenty Hands of Shield Maidens, two hundred and forty in all. Plus maybe another hundred hunters and Jarek and Kirr. "Perhaps you will see how Crow does?"

She moved away from them, toward the Shield Mothers. This would be the first real test of her command. They were in enemy territory now, and their full force still on its way. Would the Shield Mothers obey her?

Out of the corner of her eye, Milla saw Malen leave Crow's side and hurry over. The Crone was not going to let Milla talk to the Shield Mothers alone.

"I greet you, Shield Mothers," Milla announced, hurriedly closing the gap. At least she would get a few words in before Malen caught up.

"War-Chief," rumbled the reply. Some of the Shield Mothers said the title more easily than others, Milla saw.

"Come," she said. "We will take council. Ah, there is the Crone Malen. I will ask her to join us."

Since Malen was at that time only a few stretches away and obviously not to be left out, the Shield Mothers knew that this simply meant Milla was not going to wait for the Crones to tell her what to do. Some of them nodded slightly in approval, but at least as many had faint, barely impolite scowls.

They were not going to make this easy for Milla.

·CHAPTER· TWENTY-TWO

The Shield Maidens gathered around Milla in a semicircle. Malen stood with them, rather than next to Milla. Even though she didn't want the Crone to join her, Milla felt keenly alone.

They all waited for her to speak.

She ran her gaze along the Shield Mothers. She had met most of them, and knew most of their names, but not much else. Little could be told from their faces or garb. All of them wore light, in-ship furs in the colors of the Hand they led, and Selski-hide armor. Some had polished shell armor plates over the top as well. Most carried swords and spears of Selski or Wreska bone treated with the glowing algae the Crones had given them, though there were two who had bright Merwin-horn swords.

Without their face masks, they were much easier

to tell apart. They ranged in age from five or six circlings older than Milla to the vastly experienced Shield Mothers who might have had thirty or forty circlings leading Shield Maidens upon the Ice. For the latter, this would probably be their last great expedition before they went out alone to wrestle with the wind and test the warmth of the Ice against bare skin.

Milla found her throat dry and didn't know what to say. They were all staring at her, waiting. She had never imagined that this would be worse than confronting a Merwin, or escaping a Hugthing in Aenir.

But she must not show her fear. Or do any Rovkir breathing, because they would notice it. She must simply speak.

"The Chosen have been warned of our attack," she said, talking too quickly. "I think that even now they scurry back from Aenir. It was my plan to attack before they knew we were here, but that chance is lost to us now. Now I think we must make these lower levels our own, and hold them until sufficient airweed is delivered for our full host to come through the heatways."

The Shield Mothers nodded. They would not speak until Milla invited them to.

"I will show you where we are. Who has a hide

and a drawing-stick?" Milla asked. Immediately several rolled-up Wreska hides were offered to her, and a variety of writing-sticks, from basic charcoal to a thin brush and bottle of Thrill-ink.

Milla spread the hide out and knelt down, sketching quickly with the charcoal. She drew a very basic plan of the area around the Assembly, then a rough cross section of the Castle, showing the Underfolk levels and the major stairs that she knew.

"We will hold the top Underfolk level at these stairs and this ramp, and at any others that we may find, " she said, pointing to several different points. "Then the Chosen will not be able to get food or have their servants attend to them. Most of the Chosen are soft, and will suffer greatly. That will help us when the time comes for the full attack. We must move quickly to have every possible stair and way between Red One and Underfolk Seven blocked."

A Shield Mother sliced the air with her palm.

"Speak," responded Milla.

"What of the Underfolk? Will they resist?"

"Perhaps," said Milla. "But it is my wish that they are not to be harmed unless there is no other way. Some may try to go to work in the Chosen levels, but they must be turned back. We will have some

Freefolk to help explain to them, and others who will guide us."

Another Shield Mother sliced the air, one of the older ones, with many scars upon her face and hands. Milla nodded.

"This is a straight plan, War-Chief, but to make sure I have it in my old head, may I repeat it? We hold all stairs and ramps and ways between us and the Chosen, kill or capture Chosen or Spiritshadows, be wary of Underfolk but treat them well, and die before retreating."

"Yes," said Milla. "We must hold these levels, until the arrival of the main host."

Another slice through the air.

"Yes?"

"Perhaps we should speak no more, War-Chief, but hurry to find all stairs and ramps, and be ready before the enemy strikes."

Milla nodded. "This place shall be our clan-ship. Send all messengers here. Beware the shadows, for they are more dangerous than the Chosen, even with their light magic. Now, who shall go where? Speak freely."

The Shield Mothers gathered even closer, and spoke quickly, sometimes over the top of one another. But it was soon decided which Hands would go where, and as each decision was made, the relevant Shield Mother would turn away and hurry to gather her Shield Maidens and hunters.

Finally only one Shield Mother remained. The older one, with many scars. Her name was Saylsen, Milla remembered.

"I will stay here, with my Hand, to guard the ship-place and the War-Chief," said Saylsen. She glanced at Malen, and Milla caught a slight nod from the Crone. Obviously this had been decided already.

"What do the Crones say of our plans?" asked Milla. She had seen Malen's eyes go cloudy through nearly the whole meeting of the Shield Mothers.

"You are War-Chief," replied Malen, neatly avoiding an answer. Then she added, "The Freefolk boy. Crow. He is conscious. You wished to speak with him?"

"Yes!" Milla looked across at the pulpit. Sure enough, Crow was sitting up. Ferek was giving him a drink. Gill had left a little earlier, proudly leading a Hand of Shield Maidens.

Milla also saw Jarek and Kirr. They were sitting on a ledge beyond the pulpit, playing the knife-hide-stone game.

Saylsen saw her look. "Jarek and Kirr are with my Hand. The Crones asked it of them."

163

Guards, Milla thought. She wondered if they were there to protect her, or to protect Malen from her. After all, if anything happened to Malen, then Milla would be free to do as she liked, until the Crones sent a replacement.

That prompted a thought.

"Are more Crones coming?" Milla asked.

"Not until the battle is won," replied Malen. "It is not the place of a Crone to be in battle."

"What about you?" asked Milla. Malen wet her lips and looked troubled.

"You know Crones must never join any fighting. There was a lot of talk about even sending me here, where battle may come anywhere. As for the wounded —"

"Wounded live if they are meant to," interrupted Saylsen with a shrug. "If there are no Crones, there are no Crones. Warriors fight and warriors die."

"I was speaking, Shield Mother," said Malen.

Saylsen did not seem repentant. She gave Milla a look that seemed to say, *This is our business, not the Crone's.*

"Come and talk to Crow with me," said Milla to Saylsen. "He knows the Castle well, and is a sworn enemy of the Chosen."

·CHAPTER· TWENTY-THREE

The rainbow colors cleared away, leaving only a steady violet light. Tal blinked and felt the stone lid of the sarcophagus above him.

"Adras?" he whispered. He felt cool shadowflesh across his arm as Adras slid out and up the side of the sarcophagus.

"Yes?"

"Just checking," whispered Tal. "Are you all right?"

"Aenir is better than here," replied Adras. "I don't like being a shadow."

"You'll get back there," said Tal. He said it automatically, but it stuck in his head and he paused to think about what he was saying. What would he do with Adras? It was now certain that Milla was right when she said that the Chosen should not have Spiritshadows. In addition to saving the Veil, Tal would have to make sure all the Spiritshadows the Chosen now had were sent back to Aenir and made to stay there. This would include Adras.

And what would happen to the Chosen when all their Spiritshadows were gone, and — as Tal admitted had to happen — the Underfolk were freed?

Tal shook his head. Best he think like an Icecarl and worry about the Ice in front of him, not what lay behind or far ahead.

"There is something sharp . . . and hot . . . cutting into me," complained Adras. "Can we get out now?"

"Sorry," apologized Tal. It was time to act, not lie there thinking.

With Adras's help he raised the lid of the sarcophagus a fraction and looked through the gap. The Mausoleum was silent and there were no bright lights disturbing its perpetual twilight. Tal could hear a lot of shouting in the distance, but it was far off and didn't seem to be coming any closer.

He slid off the lid and climbed out. Adras flowed out after him.

The Red Keystone was lying in the sarcophagus. Tal reached in and picked it up.

"The pocket doesn't work when I'm a shadow," said Adras, rubbing his stomach.

Tal knew Spiritshadows had difficulty handling Sunstones, though they had no problem with normal items in the Dark World. He supposed it was another part of the mystery of their transformation between the worlds, the transformation that made them Spiritshadows.

Together they replaced the lid with its statue of the long-gone-to-dust occupant's Spiritshadow. Then Tal held up the Red Keystone, his forehead wrinkled in thought.

"I suppose I should release Lokar," he said, looking down at the half of the Violet Keystone on his finger. "If I can."

Adras nodded firmly. "Prison bad. Better to be free in the air."

"We'd better find somewhere to hide first," Tal said. He could still hear the shouting, and he wanted to know what was going on. But Adras was right. Now that he knew he might be able to release Lokar, he should do so as soon as possible.

The Antechamber where the Underfolk sculptors did the basic work on the statues that decorated the sarcophagi was deserted, as Tal had expected. He found a shielded spot between two columns of un-worked stone and crouched down to concentrate on the Red Keystone.

As before, he saw Lokar slowly swim into view. She was singing again, her Spiritshadow still hopping.

"Lokar!" Tal called out. "Lokar!"

She paid him no attention.

Tal called her name several times more before he realized that Lokar was particularly far gone this time. In desperation, he raised his own Sunstone until it was adjacent to the Red Keystone, so he could focus on both at once.

He didn't really know what he was doing, but he concentrated on the violet stone. Some instinct told him to try and build a wash of violet light that would flow over the Red Keystone and push its own light back.

Violet light built and started to bleed into the red of the other Keystone. As it spread, Lokar suddenly stopped singing. She looked up, stretched her hands toward Tal, and cried out.

"Highness! Release me! Release me!"

For the first time that Tal had seen, her Spirit-shadow stopped circling, too. It mirrored Lokar's actions, stretching its paws to the sky.

Violet light washed across them, a broad band against the red. Tal, still not knowing why he did it, directed it to loop behind and underneath Lokar. The light swept around her, and she threw herself into it.

The next thing Tal knew he was knocked to the ground and there was someone lying on his chest. He crawled out and gently helped Lokar up. She sobbed and clutched at him, then turned to run her hands along the stone before embracing her Spiritshadow.

Out of the Keystone, she was older and smaller than Tal had imagined she'd be. Considerably older than his mother, and only two-thirds his height, she was a tiny, fine-boned woman with short silver hair and piercing brown eyes. She wore the robes of a Brightness of the Red, but had no Sunstone. That had been taken by Sushin when she was first trapped in the Keystone.

Her Spiritshadow was larger than she was. It was a Leaper-beast, in Aenir an inhabitant of swampland and marshes. Its bulky triangular body had massive hind legs, powering impressive leaps. Its forearms were smaller, and ended in sharp claws. It also had a long and highly flexible tongue. Leaperbeasts had learned to handle basic tools with their tongues, as well as weapons. They could sling a large stone several hundred stretches, an ability the Spiritshadow form probably retained.

It took Lokar a minute to stop sobbing and regain control. She pressed her palms against her face for a moment, then straightened up and looked at Tal.

"Thank you," she said. She stared around her and added, "I saw the violet light. Where is the Empress?"

Tal bit his lip. Instead of answering, he held up his hand, with his piece of the Violet Keystone shining there.

Lokar looked puzzled, but slowly sank to one knee. She made an instinctive move to give him light, before remembering she had no Sunstone.

"I don't understand," she said. "You are Tal, aren't you? How do you come to wield the Violet Keystone?"

"You'd better stand up — or sit on that stone," Tal said. "It's kind of complicated."

As quickly as he could, he told Lokar everything that had happened since he first fell from the Red Tower. That seemed like a very long time ago.

When he had finished, Lokar looked up at the ceiling and released a long, troubled breath.

"So the Empress is dead," she said. "And Sharrakor effectively rules the Chosen through Sushin. But why has everyone come back before the Day of Dark Return?"

"I think," Tal said cautiously, "that the Icecarls might be doing something. Milla . . . Milla thought they would."

He found it hard to say the Icecarl's name. Upsetting.

"What are you going to do?" asked Lokar.

"Find my mother and give her the antidote," Tal said firmly. "Then I will climb the Orange Tower and release my father from the Keystone there. After that, I will do whatever I can to stop Sharrakor and Sushin, to save the Veil."

Lokar nodded. Then she held out her hand.

"Give me the Red Keystone. It is sealed again now. I will return it to its rightful place in the Red Tower, so it may power the Veil once more. Even if Sharrakor does manage to unseal the other Keystones, or tries to lower the Veil from the Seventh Tower, the Red Keystone will keep it going. A single Stone will keep the Veil up for seven days by itself. That may be enough, some time to buy a chance of reversal."

Tal handed her the Keystone.

"But you won't have a Sunstone once you put it back."

"I might be able to get one on the way," replied Lokar. "But even if I don't, returning the Keystone is the most important thing."

She knelt again before Tal, and gave him light from the Red Keystone, despite his attempts to raise her up.

"Don't kneel to me," he protested. "I should be kneeling to you. You're the Guardian of the Red Keystone."

"And as a Guardian I can see that you are not just the wielder, but the true Guardian of the Violet Keystone," replied Lokar. "Which means you are also Emperor of the Chosen, whether you want to be or not. Wish me light and fortune, Highness."

"Light and fortune," croaked Tal. He was Emperor of the Chosen? The boy who couldn't even get a Sunstone a few months ago?

"Light and fortune to you, Highness. And to us all."

Lokar rose and left, her Spiritshadow hopping after her as Tal stared and stared into space.

"Does that make me Emperor of all Spiritshadows?" asked Adras, who had been very interested in Lokar's obeisance.

"No," replied Tal in a faraway voice. "It doesn't make me Emperor, either, no matter what Lokar says."

He shook his head. Think like an Icecarl, he told himself. The immediate object was to get to his mother. She was probably in his family rooms, but even with all the confusion, Sushin would still make sure Graile was guarded, or there would be traps.

The first thing to do was find another disguise. A mid-ranking Chosen's robes, and he would have to work out how to stop his Sunstone being so obviously violet.

Then he would check to see exactly what was going on, and what all the panic in Aenir and the shouting here was about.

·CHAPTER·
TWENTY-FOUR

Crow was weak, but he had come back to his full senses. Ferek was helping him sip a cup of water, and telling him what had been going on. As Milla approached, Crow gently pushed the water back into Ferek's hands.

"Greetings, Crow," said Milla. She indicated the Icecarl at her right. "This is Shield Mother Saylsen, and I believe you have spoken already to the Crone Malen."

"Greetings, Milla . . . uh, that is War-Chief, and er . . . Shield Mother, and greetings again, Malen," replied Crow. His voice was scratchy, but Milla noticed another change. Crow had always almost snarled at her before, his voice permanently angry. That anger was gone. He simply sounded tired and weak.

"Has Ferek told you that I have come back with my people to put an end to the Chosen's use of Spiritshadows and save the Veil?" asked Milla. "We will help your people, too, if you let us."

"Yes," said Crow. He gave a wry smile. "I will do everything I can to help you, if you help us in return to be truly free. That is, if you don't kill me first."

"Why would we kill you?" asked Milla, puzzled.

"I mean you personally, not the Icecarls," said Crow. He stopped, took the cup from Ferek, and wet his throat before he continued. "I tried to kill your friend Tal and steal the Red Keystone."

Milla shrugged. "I've tried to kill him myself, but he survived."

"I'm serious," Crow protested. He shook his head as if he couldn't believe what he had done. "I just went crazy. I thought we had to have the Red Keystone for ourselves. Tal was a Chosen and he would always side with the Chosen. I hit him on the head, and then I threw my knife at him."

"Did you hit him?" said Milla.

"No," said Crow. "I only got his coat."

"You should practice harder."

"Is that all you have to say? I *really* tried to kill him. For no good reason. I would have gotten Ferek, Inkie, Gill . . . all of us killed if Ebbitt hadn't been there."

"It is for Tal to forgive or punish you," said Milla. She couldn't understand why Crow was so concerned. "And for you to forgive or punish him. It has nothing to do with me."

"I . . . I was rude about you," said Crow. "I insulted you, to Tal."

He looked down, unable to meet her eyes.

"Do you want to fight me?" asked Milla. She was genuinely unable to understand this Freefolk. He had fought Tal and lost, and had nearly been killed. That was all. "Speak your insults again and I will kill you. But if I have not heard them, then it is as if they have never been. They are lost on the wind."

"I don't know," whispered Crow. "I just feel . . . I feel bad."

Now Milla understood. It was the head-wound talking. When it was better, Crow would return to his usual angry self.

"We need you to look at this map," Milla said. She quickly explained what the Icecarls were trying to do, and asked Crow to point out any stairs or entrances from the Chosen levels that they might have missed.

There were quite a few. Milla marked them on her map, and wished for the perfect drawings the Codex could do. If only she'd managed to grab it before.

As each new stair, ramp, or entryway was marked, Milla and Saylsen briefly discussed how to defend or block it. Then Saylsen would send one of her Shield Maidens or hunters off to tell one of the other Shield Mothers to include the new place in her area.

Crow was still going over the map when an Ice-carl hunter burst in and came at a run toward Milla, Saylsen, and Malen. When he was a few stretches away, he clapped his fists.

"War-Chief, Shield Mother, I bring word from Shield Mother Kyal," he panted. "The Chosen have attacked. Two tens of them, with shadows, have tried to force the . . . the Red-West Roundway Down."

He stumbled on the strange place-names, but Milla had already found it on her map, her finger stabbing the hide.

"And?" she asked sharply as the hunter took a deep breath.

"We hold it," the Icecarl said proudly. "We have taken four shadows and killed three Chosen. Two of our own are wounded and one slain. Shield Mother Kyal asks for more shadow-bottles and that is all."

Milla looked at Saylsen. She did not know whether there were any such things to spare.

"Go to Anrik, there," snapped out Saylsen,

pointing. "He has four shadow-sacks. Take three. Go!"

The hunter clapped his fists and ran off.

Before anyone had a chance to say anything, another panting runner burst in from one of the closer gateways. Also a hunter, he jumped the last terrace and landed with a clatter of polished shell armor. His breastplate bore the scorch-marks of a Red Ray of Destruction. If he hadn't been wearing it, he would have been cut in half.

"War-Chief! Shield Mother Verik says more than four Hands of Chosen and shadows contest the Underfolk Watercart Ramp. They have broken through the middle gate, but we hold the lower. We need mirror-shields and shadow-sacks!"

Milla shrugged the polished shell shield off her back and gave it to him. He seemed surprised, but took it. Saylsen handed him a shadow-bottle from her own belt.

"That's it! Take them and run!"

Saylsen turned to Milla and Crow. "There were few shadow-sacks and suchlike ready for us to bring through, and I know we will need many, many more. Do you know of any other weapons here we may use against the shadows, Crow?"

Crow shook his head. "Jarnil had some shadow-sacks, like yours," he said. "But I don't know where he got them. I do have a Sunstone I can use, a little."

"As can I," said Milla. "And there is the Talon."

"The War-Chief must not fight, not unless all will be lost," said Saylsen. "The War-Chief must stand apart, for clear thought and direction."

Milla frowned and made a fist.

"That is the Crone's will, too," said Malen. As she spoke, Milla felt the words like an undigested meal in her stomach, heavy and constricting.

"But the battle has only just started, hasn't it?" asked Ferek anxiously. "And we're winning. Aren't we?"

"Yes," said Milla confidently. "We only look to what might need to be done."

Another Icecarl burst in through a different entrance. A Shield Maiden this time. She ran down the terraces and slid to a stop, speaking even as she clapped her fists together.

"War-Chief! Shield Mother Granlee reports many Chosen gathering above the Old Grand Stair. A hundred or more. Some have armor that shines in different colors, and there are many shadows. The Shield Mother says we will die bravely, but that will not be enough. She asks for another Hand or two."

"The Chosen have been much faster than I

thought," said Milla, speaking too quickly, a sure sign of her agitation. She looked at Saylsen and Malen. "A hundred Chosen, and some of them Guards. We can't risk moving any of the other Hands, in case it is just a trick. I must go!"

"No!" said Malen. The single word gripped Milla in the stomach like a vicious cramp. "It is not safe for you! Send the others, but you must stay!"

"War is not safe," snarled Saylsen angrily. "You must let the War-Chief decide for herself, Crone."

Malen looked worried. She held a hand to her temples.

"I will ask the Crone Mother. Can everyone just be quiet!"

"There is no time to ask the Crone Mother," Milla said quietly. "I *am* War-Chief of the Icecarls, Malen. I wear the Talon of Danir. Our people will not die needlessly because I would not stand with them. I *will* go."

Malen kept her hand to her temple. Her eyes began to cloud.

Milla ignored the pain in her middle and started to walk away. Saylsen walked with her, summoning her Hand with a wave. Jarek and Kirr were the first to join them, falling in behind with a passing clap of their fists.

Milla kept walking, though the pain was a fire inside her. She heard the mighty Crone voice, too, echoing inside her head. Next to her, but far enough to be out of reach of the Talon, Odris staggered through the air, clutching her stomach and her head.

Every step was agony. But Milla was too proud to give in. The Crones had decided her fate. They had laid a great task upon her. It was not a task she could complete if they tried to control everything she did from far away.

She took another step, and another. Sweat poured from her face and her skin went whiter than the purest snow. But she was almost at her limit of pain and strength. Another few steps and she would fall.

She lifted her foot and slid it forward. As the pain increased, and the great Crone voice inside her head crescendoed, she heard Malen's soft voice cut through pain and noise.

"Go, War-Chief. The Crones say you are free. Free to fight as you think best."

·CHAPTER·
TWENTY–FIVE

In the same laundry holding area he'd used before, Tal found the robes of a Brightstar of the Yellow Order. After he changed into them, he added a bandage around his head. That would not be seen as too unusual right at the moment, Tal thought, as he listened to the continued shouting and the distant sound of what had to be fighting echoing up the laundry chute.

Adras was disguised, too. Tal helped him take on the appearance of a slightly malnourished Borzog, pulling at the Spiritshadow's shoulders and arms. Eventually Adras had the shape almost right.

The Violet Keystone took a little more work to camouflage. It simply didn't want to change color, and Tal had to use all his willpower to get it to revert to its former colors. Eventually he managed it, and it stayed yellow with flecks of red.

He was also pleased to find a packet of dried shrimps in another set of robes. While there was no real need to eat in Aenir, he couldn't remember when he'd last eaten in his normal body. The shrimps went down in a few quick gulps, accompanied by a long drink of water from the prewashing sink used by the Underfolk laundry people.

Disguised, and fortified with food, Tal ventured out into the main Yellow levels. Chosen were hurrying everywhere, yelling and carrying on, and there were a few Underfolk trying to go about their business. Tal kept his head down and walked slowly, as if he were injured.

It took Tal a while to realize that he was going against the tide of traffic. He was headed down to the Orange levels. Most of the Chosen were heading up, many of them with their Spiritshadows carrying their valuables, children behind them with their shadowguards carrying their toys and keepsakes.

But not all Chosen were fleeing what Tal guessed was a battle with the Icecarls. He had to press himself against the wall of a colorless through-corridor as a disciplined troop of Guards jogged past, side by side with their thin-waisted Spiritshadows. Behind them hurried twenty or thirty determined-looking Chosen of all Orders, Red to Violet, carrying improvised weapons and many Sunstones. Their Spiritshadows danced around them, up and down the walls and across the ceiling. Tal checked them out from the corner of his eye, but couldn't see any extras. So far the free Spiritshadows in the Castle seemed to be biding their time.

As the Guards went past, Tal took the opportunity to slide along to another Chosen, a Brightblinder of the Blue, who had also moved out of the way.

"What is the news?" asked Tal. He didn't bother to give light in respect. Nobody else was, either. Proper courtesy seemed to be the first thing to go.

"The same as before," remarked the Chosen. "Vicious monsters in the lower levels, with white faces. The Guards will sort them out."

He said the last without absolute confidence.

"What of the Empress?" asked Tal.

The Brightblinder stared at him without comprehension.

"She has announced that the weapons of the Seventh Tower will be used against the invaders," he said. "Is that what you mean?"

"No," said Tal. What were the weapons of the Seventh Tower? "No. I heard she was . . . I heard she was sick."

The Brightblinder shook his head. "I've heard all sorts of things today, but nothing as stupid as that. Hold! Where are you going?"

Tal had started to edge away, to follow the Guards.

"That's not the way, Brightstar! Hasn't your Lumenor told you where to report? We're clearing out everything from Indigo down!"

Tal didn't answer. He tried to look vacant and staggered across the traffic, which had resumed going the other way. He earned some angry cries, but by the time he'd threaded his way through, the Brightblinder was lost in the sea of fleeing Chosen.

After that, Tal took lesser-known ways down to the Orange levels. The Brightblinder had obviously known what he was talking about, as the lower Tal went, the more deserted it was. There were still Guards and irregular groups of Chosen with them heading down, but Tal stayed out of their way or pretended to be resting before continuing on up. In any case they were always in too much of a hurry to pay any attention to him.

Finally, he came to the familiar Orange levels that had been home for most of his life. They did not feel like home now. Tal realized he didn't really feel like a Chosen anymore, either. Certainly he had no desire either to join those fleeing upward, or the fighters heading down.

At the corner of the corridor that led to his family's rooms, Tal paused. He looked down it and saw the familiar door with his family's sigil. The orange Sthil-beast leaping over a seven-pointed star.

His eyes misted as he remembered rushing home when he first got the news of his father's disappearance. He had tried not to cry then, not wanting anyone to see his sorrow and fear. Sushin had been waiting inside.

It was unlikely Sushin was waiting inside now, not with the Icecarls attacking. But Tal was sure he would have left traps, and perhaps free shadows, to guard Graile. He had almost caught Tal before in a similar way, by using his brother, Gref, as bait.

"You see the door with the Sthil-beast?" Tal whispered to Adras. "Can you slide under and have a look around? Be careful. There might be traps, or enemies."

"Adras will break traps and tear enemies into three," declared the Spiritshadow.

"In half, I think you mean," corrected Tal.

"No, three. One piece left, one piece right, one

piece to trample on," said Adras. "It is the Storm Shepherd way. That's what Odris is doing now."

"Odris?" asked Tal. His voice sort of squeaked, in either nervousness or excitement. "She's in the Castle?"

Adras nodded and pointed one massive thumb at the floor.

"Down below. Fighting. I hear the wind tell me."

"And Milla?" Tal asked eagerly. "Is she still alive?"

"Don't know," said Adras. "Wind speaks only of Odris. But wind would not know Milla anyway."

"Maybe Milla's showing the Icecarls the way in," Tal said quietly. "They would need a guide, and she's the obvious choice. Maybe they wouldn't let her go to the Ice because she was needed."

Adras shrugged. He didn't know. He was happy to know Odris was close. He would see her soon.

Tal felt happier, too. He'd never really believed that Milla was dead, but he'd feared that she was. But if Odris was here, and fighting with the Icecarls . . .

"Do I go now?" interrupted Adras.

"Yes, yes!" said Tal. "But be careful. Unlock the door if it's locked, and don't touch anything suspicious."

Adras drifted down the corridor. Tal watched

anxiously as he slid under the door, every sense alert. But he didn't hear anything, and there was no sign of any alarm or trap.

Minutes passed. Adras did not return. Tal stayed crouched at the corner, tension mounting inside him. What had happened to the Spiritshadow?

Another minute passed. Tal stood up, crouched down, stood up again.

Another minute passed. Tal pushed his Sunstone ring up and down his finger nervously. Surely Adras would have opened the door by now? Something must have gone wrong.

Tal started to sneak along the corridor, his Sunstone hand held ready. Red light started to billow to the surface of the stone, as Tal prepared a Red Ray of Destruction.

He was almost at the door when it suddenly swung open. For a split second, Tal was about to fire the Red Ray at whatever came out. But he didn't, because it was Adras.

"What are you waiting for?" asked the Spiritshadow. "I unlocked the door ages ago. There's no one here anyway. Just one of your lot, sound asleep in a funny hot room at the back."

"That's not 'one of my lot,'" Tal said angrily. "That's my mother!"

·CHAPTER·
TWENTY-SIX

Milla danced a dance of death, the Talon's whip of light weaving around her like a razor-sharp ribbon. She mowed through the ranks of attacking Spiritshadows like a Merwin through a half-asleep herd of Wreska.

As the Talon cut, sliced, and choked through the Spiritshadows, it also deflected the rays of light and other magics that were sent against the War-Chief of the Icecarls. But quick as it was, faster than a Fleamite, the Talon could not fully deflect every Red Ray or Blue Burst the Chosen was firing from their makeshift barricade higher up the wide reaches of the Old Grand Stair.

Red light struck and Milla was lightly burned across both arms. But she did not fall back until the Spiritshadows were in full retreat. Even then, the

Talon tried to lash out behind Milla, and she only just managed to turn it aside as Odris grabbed her and dragged her back behind the Icecarls' own wall of partially reflective crystal panels, stacked against a breastwork of barrels, boxes, and anything else they could drag up from the Underfolk level at the end of the stair.

As Odris dragged Milla away, several Shield Maidens paused in their own retreat to raise their mirror-shields to guard the War-Chief. They did it not a moment too soon, as more Red Rays and an Indigo Cutter zapped down, blowing chips of stone out of the steps as they were deflected by the shields.

Momentarily safe behind the barricade, Milla and Odris hunkered down as about a dozen hunters stood up and hurled their glowing spears at the last few Spiritshadows.

Saylsen crept up to them, her head just below the level of the barricade. More Red Rays crisscrossed overhead as she approached.

"Well done, War-Chief!" exclaimed the old Shield Mother. "If only the cowards themselves would attack, instead of sending their shadows! Then we would show them!"

Milla set her teeth for a moment, as she began to feel the pain from her burns.

"They show good sense," she said grimly. "The Spiritshadows do not die easily, and their Chosen masters will survive their pain. I wish that we had Spiritshadows to die for us."

She looked around. They had been fighting on the stair for almost a Chosen hour by her Sunstone, and there had been many deaths and many wounded among the Icecarls.

"There is no honor here," Milla added. It was not like the old stories and legends. "There is only foul and unpleasant work that must be done."

She saw Malen tending to a dying Shield Maiden, and crawled down to her.

"What news of the main host?" asked Milla.

Malen shook her head. Her hands were shaking, Milla saw.

"I . . . I don't know," Malen whispered. "I can't hear them in the middle of this. I can't hear them!"

"It doesn't matter," Milla calmed her. "Just do what you can for the wounded. I've sent runners back. They will bring up the others when they come."

When they come, Milla thought. She hoped it would be soon enough. Even with the Talon, there was a limit to how many Spiritshadows they could stop. There had been six assaults so far down the stairs. Each time there had been more Spiritshadows, and each time they had been barely thrown back.

Milla looked across at the end of the barricade, where there was a considerable space after the main body of defenders. Everywhere else the line was packed tight with Shield Maidens and hunters, staying low until they had to confront the next attack.

The reason for the space was immediately clear. Jarek was there, staring through a slight gap between two panes of crystal. His vast blue-stained chest was rising and falling like a bellows, and he held his great chain of gold metal taut between two huge fists. Kirr was stroking the back of his neck and whispering in his ear. She had managed to get him to come back after each attack, a feat Milla would have believed impossible after seeing his intense rage and the carnage he wreaked among the Spiritshadows with his chain. The golden metal, like certain types of light, was all too solid to Spiritshadows.

As Milla watched, a Red Ray drilled through the gap and struck Jarek on the chest. Anyone else would have been killed instantly, but his skin, soaked in Norrworm blood, reflected the ray. It hit a barrel and sliced away a long wooden splinter.

The splinter flew through the air with an awful whir, and went straight into Kirr.

The Shield Maiden fell without a sound, crumpled over the next lower step. Milla ran to her, as fast as she could without exposing herself. Malen followed, her slim medicine pack in hand.

Even before they got there, they knew nothing could be done. The splinter was as long as an arrow, and by terrible mischance it had struck Kirr under the arm, where she had no armor.

Jarek looked down at his partner and touched her gently on the back. When she did not move, he rolled her over. Milla and Malen froze, seeing the madness in his eyes.

Jarek put Kirr down again. His head went back, and he gave the most terrible howl anyone had ever heard, Icecarl or Chosen. It was louder and fiercer than a Merwin's screech, deeper than the distant rumble of the Selski.

Time stood still. Even the Chosen stopped firing Red Rays over the barricade.

Jarek rose up and smashed his way through the barricade, whirling the great chain above his head. The awful howl continued, far longer than anyone's lungs could have sustained it.

Red Rays flashed and played across his body, but

he did not fall back. A Blue Burst broke over him, but he did not falter.

Milla didn't need to think twice.

"Attack!" she yelled. "For Kirr! Attack!"

In an instant, every Icecarl was up, including many wounded. The barricade was pushed aside or jumped or bulled through, as every Shield Maiden and hunter stormed up the stairs in the wake of the Wilder Jarek's chain and War-Chief Milla's terrible Talon.

·CHAPTER·
TWENTY–SEVEN

Tal advanced into the antechamber cautiously. Despite Adras's complacency, he was sure there was a trap. There was no way Sushin would have left Graile unguarded.

But he couldn't see anything. There were no strange Sunstones in the walls or ceiling. No shadows moving where they shouldn't be, no odd patches of darkness.

He checked the door to the sunroom. Adras had opened it, and it, too, seemed innocuous.

Tal edged through the doorway, ready for anything. As always, the heat hit him, and the humidity. The sunroom's walls and ceiling were covered in tiny Sunstones that constantly emitted light and heat. The humidity was explained by an onion-shaped dome in the corner, pricked with thousands of tiny holes that had steam wafting out of them. It was directly connected to one of the lesser steam pipes of the Castle.

Graile was lying on the bed, not moving. Tal felt a sharp pain in his chest as he saw her. She looked so gray and wasted. For a panicked second he couldn't see her Spiritshadow, then he spotted it under the bed. It, too, had faded, and was now only a sad remnant of the great shadow owl it had once been.

Tal stood absolutely still, looking at his sick mother. Was it water-spider venom that had made her like this? Water-spider venom given to her by Sushin? Or was it something else, something that the antidote he now clutched in his hand would be useless against?

Tal took a deep breath and knelt down by the bed. He opened the vial of antidote, then gently lifted Graile's head, supporting her neck. She was breathing very, very slowly and infrequently, and she did not respond to his touch. Her skin was also very, very cold.

Tal poured the antidote into her mouth, closed it, pinched her nose, and shook her a little.

For a few seconds nothing happened. Then she suddenly coughed, an explosive cough that almost made Tal let go of her. He did release his pinch on her nose.

She coughed again, a racking cough that shook her whole body. Then her eyes opened. She couldn't focus at first.

Tal eased her head back onto the pillows. Her eyes grew sharp, and she smiled at him as he plumped up her pillows.

"Tal," she whispered. "You've grown."

Tal smiled back, and a single tear slid down his cheek. He wiped it away as Graile saw the ring upon his hand.

"You've got a Sunstone," she added, her voice so faint Tal could hardly hear. "A Primary Sunstone. We will be able to go to Aenir."

Her own Sunstone lay on her chest, suspended on a silver chain. It barely sparked. Tal wondered what Sushin had done to it.

"It's a bit more complicated than that, Mother," Tal said hastily. He looked around. He knew Sushin must have trapped the room somehow. "A lot has happened. A real lot. We have to get away from here, for a start."

Graile nodded, but when she tried to get up it was obviously beyond her. Her Spiritshadow, which was also looking a little better, tried to help her, but it still had no strength.

"Adras will carry you," said Tal. "My Spiritshadow. Adras!"

"Your Spiritshadow!" echoed Graile. She smiled again. "A lot has happened."

"Adras!"

Adras came back into the room. He was holding a tiny, squirming fleck of shadow in two fingers.

"Look what I found. There were lots of them, but the others got away."

Tal stared at the tiny wriggling thing. It was the smallest Spiritshadow he had ever seen. He couldn't even clearly see what it was.

"It's the Spiritshadow of a Frox," explained Adras kindly. "This is what a swarm's made out of."

"It's speaking aloud," said Graile faintly. Tal thought she meant the Frox, until he realized she meant Adras. Chosen Spiritshadows never spoke in public. Only to their masters, in private.

"Adras is different," said Tal quickly. The Frox that got away were probably reporting to someone right now. They had to move quickly.

"Adras, please pick up my mother carefully," he said. "Her name is Graile. You must protect her as if she were me."

"Sure," boomed Adras. He bent over the bed and easily picked up both Graile and her Spiritshadow, which jumped onto her stomach at the last moment. In full health, the great owl was normally the same size as Tal. But it had withered to less than a third of his height.

"Where are we going?" whispered Graile. "How did you wake me?"

"You've been poisoned with water-spider venom," explained Tal quickly as he led the way out. "I got an antidote from . . . from Ebbitt . . . um . . . I'll explain . . . that is . . ."

A sound from beyond the outer door saved him. Footsteps.

Tal raised his Sunstone. All his anxiety and fear for his mother flowed into it. The stone took it in as raw power, and instantly shed its disguise.

Violet light filled the room. Graile let out a shocked cry.

"Violet!"

Tal cursed.

Someone tried the door.

"Back!" Tal whispered. They retreated swiftly back. Tal paused at the sunroom door, keeping it open a fraction. His Sunstone, now a vivid violet, shone ready. Once again, Tal didn't have a particular Light spell ready. Just a violent anger that he let build in the Sunstone.

The outer door opened. Two Guards crept in. They had their swords and Sunstones ready.

Sushin was behind them, his great bulk filling the door. He was wearing the robes of a Violet Shadowlord openly, and had even more Sunstones on his hands and body than ever before.

Tal didn't wait. He directed all his hatred through the Sunstone and out toward the three Chosen.

A terrible blast of raw violet light flew across the room. It blew furniture to pieces, picked up the Guards, and hurled them out into the corridor.

The blast sent Sushin reeling back, his Sunstones flashing as they absorbed the shock. Before Tal could loose another blast, Sushin threw something at him. A ball, about the size of a juice-fruit.

It hit Tal on the chest, and exploded everywhere exactly like a juice-fruit. Water flew up in Tal's face and dripped down his chin. But water tainted with something, something that smelled horrible and familiar. Tal couldn't place it for a moment. Then he knew.

It was spider venom!

A second later, Tal felt it flow through his veins. It might be slower than when it was injected by a spider, but he probably had less than a minute before he would be unconscious.

He slammed the door and staggered back. Adras was putting Graile down on the bed, the big Spirit-shadow already yawning.

"Mother!" Tal said, forcing the words out against the darkness that was descending inside his head. "Pretend to be sick still. When you can, go down to the Underfolk levels. Tell the Icecarls you're Tal's mother. Tell them to take you to Milla, if she lives. Tell her Lokar is released. Take the violet half . . ."

He tried to slip the Sunstone from his finger, but it was already too late. It was on too tight, and there was no strength in his hands. Then he remembered the last vial of antidote, still tied into his shirt.

Weakening fingers fumbled at the knot.

He almost had it undone when darkness claimed him.